JOHN KUYKENDALL

The Last Dawn

SQUATCH GQ
PUBLISHING CO

Contents

Chapter 10: The Road Ahead

Dedication

To the survivors, those who have faced the unimaginable and still found the strength to rise. To those who remember, who hold onto the flickering embers of hope in the face of darkness. This story is for you.

Preface

The world ended in a fiery symphony of destruction. The echoes of that cataclysmic event still resonate in the desolate landscapes that remain. Yet, from the ashes, a new chapter unfolds – a testament to the indomitable spirit of humanity.

This story is born from those ashes. It is a tale of resilience, a testament to the enduring power of the human spirit. It is a journey into the heart of a broken world, where survival is a daily struggle, and trust a precious commodity.

But it is also a journey into the heart of ourselves, into the depths of our own humanity. For in the face of unimaginable despair, we are forced to confront the darkness within, to make choices that will define us forever.

The events that follow are a stark reflection of the chaos that engulfed the world. The characters you will meet are not heroes in the traditional sense. They are ordinary people thrust into extraordinary circumstances, grappling with the weight of loss, the burden of survival, and the ever-present threat of betrayal.

Their journey is not a simple quest for redemption. It is a relentless struggle for truth, a desperate search for answers to a horrifying question: what truly happened? And what will become of the world – and us – in its wake?

Introduction

The air hangs heavy with the scent of decay. The silence is broken only by the creaking of rusted metal and the mournful wind whispering through the skeletal remains of once-proud skyscrapers. This is the world now, a testament to the destructive power of human ambition.

But amidst the rubble, amidst the despair, there is a flicker of life. Lila, a

resourceful scavenger, emerges from the ruins, haunted by the ghosts of her past. Her life before the apocalypse is a blurry memory, overshadowed by the crushing weight of loss and the constant struggle for survival.

She has learned to adapt, to make do with what little remains. But she is also driven by a thirst for answers, an insatiable hunger for truth that she knows lies buried beneath the layers of destruction. She is not alone in her search. A small group of survivors, each with their own burdens and their own reasons for seeking a better future, forms a fragile alliance with Lila.

Together, they will face the perils of a broken world – mutated creatures, roving gangs, and the ever-present threat of betrayal. They will confront the ghosts of their past, the dark whispers of a forgotten conspiracy, and the enduring question that haunts them all: what is left to hope for in a world on the brink of oblivion?

This journey is not about the ending. It is about the journey itself, the choices we make when everything we know is gone, and the strength we find within

ourselves to survive. It is a story of the last dawn, the faint

3

glimmer of hope that refuses to be extinguished, even in the darkest of times.

The Ruins of a Life

Chapter 1: The Echo of Ashes

The world outside her window was a canvas of gray, a desolate landscape painted with the muted hues of despair. The city, once a bustling metropolis, was now a graveyard of broken dreams, its skeletal structures reaching towards a sky choked with dust and ash. Lila, perched precariously on the edge of a crumbling building, scanned the horizon with the practiced eye of a survivor. The city was her domain, its ruins her hunting ground.

A decade had passed since the bombs fell, painting the world in shades of gray and etching the memory of that fateful day into her very soul. The world had been ripped apart, leaving behind a symphony of screams and the lingering stench of death. She had been a child then, her innocence shattered by the violence that consumed her world. She had seen her brother, his laughter forever silenced by the unrelenting fury of the bombs. The image of his lifeless eyes, staring up at the sky that had betrayed them, haunted her nights.

Her parents, she could only imagine, were lost in the chaos. Perhaps they had found solace in the arms of a fiery inferno, their cries swallowed by the roar of destruction. The world had been reborn in flames, leaving behind a wasteland that tested the limits of human endurance. The survivors, like her, were mere specks in the vast canvas of desolation, fighting to keep their flickering hope alive.

She had learned to survive, to adapt to the harsh realities of the world that had been reborn in the throes of destruction. The once-familiar streets had become her classroom, teaching her the language of survival, the art of scavenging, and the art of disappearing into the shadows. She was a phantom, a whisper in the wind, moving through the ruins with a grace that was born of necessity.

The remnants of the old world, the debris of a forgotten civilization, were her treasure trove. She knew where to find the hidden caches of food, the forgotten water reservoirs, the scattered tools that could be repurposed for survival. The world had become a puzzle, and she had learned to piece it together, to find beauty in the broken, to carve out a semblance of life in the ruins.

She was a survivor, a testament to human resilience, a solitary figure in a world that had lost its heart. The haunting echoes of the past, the whispers of a life lost, were a constant companion, a reminder of what she had lost and what she was fighting to reclaim. But she was also a hunter, a predator in a world where every day was a battle for survival, and every encounter a potential threat.

Her senses were sharpened, her instincts honed, her movements fluid and precise. The silence of the ruins was her language, the debris her camouflage. She was a ghost, a whisper in the wind, a fleeting shadow in the ruins of a world that had forgotten what it meant to be alive. The world had lost its colors, but she clung to the faint hope that it was possible to reclaim the beauty that had been stolen.

Her heart, a fragile vessel, held a flicker of light, a spark of defiance against the darkness that threatened to consume her. She wasn't just scavenging for survival; she was searching for a shred of purpose, a reason to keep going. It was a hope, however faint, that propelled her forward, urging her to delve deeper into the heart of the ruins, to uncover the truth that lay buried beneath the ashes.

Whispers of Conspiracy

Lila's fingers, calloused and strong from years of scavenging, traced the faded inscription etched onto the rusted metal of the old signpost. It read: "Welcome to Eden." A bitter chuckle escaped her lips. Eden. This desolate wasteland, choked with the ghosts of a forgotten past, couldn't be further from a paradise.

The inscription wasn't the only thing that piqued her interest.

On the back of the signpost, almost hidden by layers of grime, was a barely discernible symbol: a circle bisected by a diagonal line, ending in a jagged point. She recognized it.

It was a symbol she'd seen before, scrawled on the crumbling walls of abandoned buildings, whispered in the hushed tones of those who dared to speak of what happened.

It was a symbol of the conspiracy, a whisper of a truth that had been buried under the ashes of the world. The whispers had always been there, a persistent echo of doubt in the aftermath of the catastrophe. They spoke of a world consumed by chaos, not through a random accident, but through a carefully orchestrated event.

Lila had always dismissed them as the ramblings of the

desperate, a coping mechanism for the unimaginable pain.

But the symbol, the way it seemed to taunt her from the depths of the wasteland, sent a shiver down her spine. It stirred something deep within her, a restless echo of curiosity, a burning need for answers.

Days turned into weeks as Lila followed the trail of whispers, her journey taking her through landscapes scarred by the apocalypse. Every crumbling building, every

abandoned outpost seemed to hold a piece of the puzzle, a fragment of a forgotten story. Each new discovery fueled her determination, pushing her further into the heart of the conspiracy.

One afternoon, as she scavenged through the debris of a collapsed building, she stumbled upon a hidden compartment. Inside, she found a tattered notebook, its pages filled with scribbled notes and sketches. It was the journal of a scientist, someone who had witnessed the events leading to the apocalypse firsthand.

The scientist's words, penned with a mix of despair and fury, painted a harrowing picture. He spoke of a government project, code-named "The Last Dawn," that had been shrouded in secrecy. The project, he alleged, was a calculated attempt to reshape the world, using a devastating weapon that had been unleashed upon humanity with devastating consequences.

The notebook confirmed what Lila had always suspected, but it also raised new questions. Who had authorized the project? Why? And most importantly, was there anyone left who could expose the truth and hold those responsible accountable?

The weight of the discovery pressed down on Lila, an

oppressive sense of responsibility that mirrored the

oppressive blanket of ash that covered the world. The weight of the truth, she realized, was a heavy burden to bear, but she couldn't ignore it. She had to find a way to bring the light of truth to the world shrouded in darkness.

She continued her journey, each step fueled by a newfound purpose. The whispers had morphed into a chorus, a

symphony of unanswered questions, a desperate plea for justice. She was no longer just a scavenger, a survivor

scraping by in the ruins of the old world. She was a seeker of truth, a harbinger of a possible future where the truth could be brought to light.

Along her journey, she stumbled upon a small group of survivors, gathered around a flickering fire in the heart of an abandoned town. They were a ragtag band of individuals, each bearing their own scars of the apocalypse. But despite the hardship they had endured, they held onto a flicker of hope, a belief that a better future was still possible.

Their leader, a charismatic and resilient man named Ethan, offered Lila a place among them. He listened to her stories of the conspiracy, his eyes gleaming with a shared desire for answers. He believed in the power of truth, and he saw in Lila a kindred spirit, a fellow seeker of justice.

Lila felt a glimmer of hope rekindle within her. For the first time since the apocalypse, she found herself surrounded by people who shared her thirst for justice, who yearned for a world free from the shadows of deception. She realized that she wasn't alone in her quest for answers, and the burden she carried suddenly felt a little lighter.

Ethan and his group, they became her companions, her allies

in the face of a world shrouded in lies. Together, they
ventured into the heart of the conspiracy, following the trail
of clues, their journey taking them through landscapes
scarred by the apocalypse.

But the path to truth, Lila soon realized, was a treacherous
one. Every step forward was met with new obstacles, every
revelation brought new dangers. And the threat wasn't just
from the remnants of a shattered world, but from the
shadows of human nature itself.

One night, during their journey, a member of their group, a

young woman named Maya, disappeared. They searched for her,
their hearts heavy with worry, but she was gone. The discovery
of a single, bloody knife in the desolate landscape confirmed
their fears. Maya was gone, taken by something, or someone,
lurking in the darkness.

The loss of Maya shook their group, exposing the cracks in
their unity. The once-bright flicker of hope began to dwindle,
replaced by a cold wave of suspicion. Whispers of betrayal
swirled around the campfire, the seeds of doubt planted in the
fertile soil of fear and grief.

Lila felt the weight of distrust pressing down on her. She knew
that the dangers they faced were not just from the world outside
but from the darkness that could bloom even within their own
hearts. She knew they were no longer just fighting for survival,
but also for the preservation of their own humanity in a world
that seemed determined to tear it apart.

As they continued their journey, the weight of Maya's
absence and the simmering tension within the group pushed
them towards a turning point. They knew they had to find
answers, not just about the conspiracy, but about themselves.

They had to find a way to navigate the treacherous waters of suspicion and betrayal, to find strength in their shared desire for truth and their fragile hope for a better future.

Lila knew that the road ahead would be long and perilous, but she was determined to keep moving forward. She had seen too much darkness, too much despair, to let it consume her. She would not let the whispers of the past silence the cries for justice, for a new dawn, for a world where truth could finally prevail.

A Glimpse of Hope

The sun, a pale, watery orb, struggled to pierce the thick, gray haze that hung over the ruins. It was a world of broken glass, twisted metal, and the silent, accusing ghosts of buildings that had once scraped the sky. Lila, her face obscured by a ragged scarf, her eyes narrowed against the dust that danced in the wind, navigated the rubble-strewn streets with the practiced ease of a seasoned survivor.

For years, this desolation had been her only home, the jagged remains of civilization her only companions. The memories of the Day – the day the world had ended – still burned with an almost unbearable intensity. The screams, the fire, the blinding flash of light, the suffocating darkness that followed... it all felt like a nightmare that refused to fade.

A flicker of movement caught her eye. In the distance, near the skeletal remains of what had once been a sprawling supermarket, a plume of smoke rose into the air. A fire. A sign of life.

As she approached, the faint smell of burning wood mixed with the metallic tang of decay. The fire was small, contained within a makeshift enclosure of rusted metal sheets. Around it, huddled figures, their faces etched with the harsh realities of survival.

A man, tall and lean with piercing blue eyes, emerged from the shadows. He wore a tattered leather jacket over a worn, but clean, cotton shirt. He offered Lila a small, but reassuring smile.

"Welcome, stranger," he said, his voice a low rumble that

seemed to carry the weight of the world. "We haven't seen a new face in a while."

"Just passing through," Lila said cautiously, her hand instinctively resting on the worn leather of her makeshift scabbard, where her rusty blade lay nestled.

"We're called the Wanderers," the man continued, "Ethan's the name." He gestured toward the others. "These are Maya, she's our healer, and Jacob, our tracker."

They each offered a nod, their faces weary but their eyes holding a glimmer of something... something hopeful.

Lila couldn't help but notice the way they moved, a sense of purpose and teamwork that was foreign to her solitary existence. They weren't just surviving; they were striving.

Ethan offered her a ration of dry biscuits and a lukewarm cup of water from a battered thermos.

"We were out gathering firewood," Ethan explained, "and saw your smoke."

"I had to start a fire to boil some water," Lila said, her voice raspy from disuse. "Been feeling a bit under the weather."

"A touch of the sickness?" Maya asked, her voice gentle, laced with concern. "It's going around, but we've managed to hold it at bay with herbs and some good old fashioned care."

Lila nodded, surprised by their kindness. She hadn't encountered such warmth and hospitality in years. The world seemed to be filled with suspicion and distrust. It had been a long time since she had felt this sense of... belonging.

As the fire crackled and the night fell, they shared their

stories, their voices weaving a tapestry of survival, resilience, and hope. Lila learned that they were a group of survivors, drawn together by a shared desire for a better future. They were searching for a place to start anew, a place where they could rebuild and create a life worth living.

Ethan spoke about his vision of a new world, a world where communities thrived and resources were shared. He spoke of the whispers of rumors, about a hidden haven, a place rumored to be untouched by the devastation.

"We have to believe in a future," Ethan said, his eyes gleaming with a fierce conviction. "The world is broken, yes, but the human spirit... that still burns bright."

His words touched a deep, forgotten place within Lila. For the first time since the Day, a flicker of hope, a faint but persistent spark, ignited within her. Perhaps the world wasn't entirely lost. Perhaps, amidst the ashes, there was still a chance for a new beginning.

As the fire dwindled and the stars began to emerge, a feeling of comfort settled over Lila. The weight of her solitary existence, the burden of her past, seemed to lighten just a little. For the first time in a long time, she felt a sense of connection, a sense of belonging to something larger than herself.

In the cold, unforgiving world, she had found a glimmer of warmth, a beacon of hope. Maybe, just maybe, the echo of ashes wasn't the end, but the beginning.

The First Betrayal

The air hung heavy with the scent of decay and ash, a grim reminder of the world that had been. The fire had finally died down, leaving behind a pile of smoldering embers that mirrored the hollowness gnawing at Lila's insides. She watched the flickering flames, a silent witness to the betrayal that had shattered their fragile sense of unity.

It had started with a whisper, a misplaced glance, a subtle shift in the dynamics of their small, tattered family. Elias, the man who had initially welcomed them with open arms, had become a shadow, his eyes darting with a new, unsettling intensity. Lila had dismissed it as paranoia, a symptom of the world's relentless pressure, but a deep, instinctive unease had taken root within her.

It was the way he lingered around their meager supplies, the way his hand lingered a moment too long on the worn map detailing their route. The tension had escalated as they ventured deeper into the desolate wasteland, their supplies dwindling with each passing day. They had stumbled upon a hidden cache of food and water, a meager bounty in a world where even the most basic necessities were scarce. Elias, always the charismatic leader, had rallied the group, praising their luck.

But Lila noticed a flicker of greed in his eyes, a predatory gleam that made her skin crawl. The trust that had been carefully woven, thread by thread, began to unravel, frayed by doubt and suspicion. That night, as they huddled around a crackling fire, Elias, his face contorted with a mixture of desperation and malice, announced his intention to leave. He claimed it was for their safety, that he had received

information about a potential danger lurking on their path.

But Lila knew better. The truth, like a festering wound, pulsed beneath the surface of his words. He wanted the supplies, the coveted resources they had found. He wanted to survive, even if it meant leaving the others to face the unforgiving wasteland alone.

Her heart pounded against her ribs, a drumbeat of fear and anger. She saw the raw terror in the eyes of the others, their hopes collapsing like a house of cards. Their fragile unity shattered, leaving them vulnerable, exposed to the cruel whims of a world that seemed determined to tear them apart.

The betrayal had been swift and brutal, a sharp blade cutting through the thin fabric of trust that held them together. It exposed the dark underbelly of human nature, the primal instincts that lurked beneath the veneer of civilization.

Survival, in this desolate world, was a brutal game, and Elias, with his calculated betrayal, had shown them that no bond, not even the shared struggle for survival, could withstand the insidious lure of self-preservation.

The remaining survivors, their spirits bruised and their trust shattered, were left to face the unforgiving wasteland alone. They looked at each other, the faces etched with a mixture of anger, sorrow, and a lingering flicker of hope. Lila, her heart heavy with betrayal, knew they had to move on. The road ahead was treacherous, but they couldn't afford to let the echoes of Elias's treachery consume them. They had to keep going, to find their strength, to find their purpose, to find a way to rebuild, not just their lives, but their faith in humanity.

The Journey Begins

The air hung heavy with the scent of ash and decay, a

constant reminder of the world that had been. Lila, her face smudged with grime, surveyed the desolate landscape before her. Twisted metal skeletons of buildings reached for the sky, their hollow windows like vacant eyes staring into a bleak future. The once vibrant city was now a graveyard of

shattered dreams, a testament to the devastation that had swept across the land.

Lila had learned to navigate this post-apocalyptic world, her senses honed to the subtleties of survival. She was a ghost in the ruins, moving with a fluidity that belied the weight of the past she carried. The memory of the day the world ended was etched in her mind, a vivid tableau of fire, chaos, and the piercing scream of her brother as he vanished in the maelstrom.

The whisper of a conspiracy had been the catalyst, a cryptic message scrawled on a tattered piece of paper found tucked inside a rusted toolbox. It spoke of a hidden truth, a dark secret that lay buried beneath the ashes of the apocalypse. The message was a seed of hope, a flicker in the darkness, urging her to seek the truth, even if it meant venturing into the unknown.

As she traversed the ruins, her ears were attuned to the faintest of sounds - the rustle of wind through shattered windows, the distant rumble of a mutated creature, the echoing footsteps of other survivors. She was not alone in this desolate world, but the encounters were often fraught with danger, a constant reminder of the fragility of life.

The first flicker of genuine hope came when she stumbled upon a group of survivors huddled around a dying fire. They were a motley crew, their faces weathered by hardship, their eyes reflecting a blend of fear and defiance. At their heart stood Ethan, a man with a charisma that drew Lila in. His voice resonated with a quiet strength, his words promising a semblance of normalcy in a world that had lost its bearings.

Ethan's group, known as the "Echoes", offered Lila a sense of belonging she had long craved. Their shared desire for survival, for understanding the truth, was a powerful bond that drew them together. They had a sense of purpose, a mission that transcended the mere act of surviving.

Their first challenge, however, was the betrayal of a trusted member, a man known as Marcus, who had been welcomed into their circle with open arms. Marcus was a man of

contradictions, a skilled hunter with a sly smile that hinted at a darker side. His treachery was swift and brutal, a reminder that in a world where resources were scarce and trust a

luxury, even those closest to you could turn into enemies.

Lila, with a heart heavy with betrayal and a mind steeled with resolve, chose to stay with the Echoes. They were her family now, and she was determined to see their journey through. They were united by a common purpose - to

unravel the secrets of the apocalypse, to find the truth, and to bring justice to those responsible for the devastation that had consumed their world.

The journey was fraught with danger. The landscape was a tapestry of shattered roads, crumbling buildings, and

desolate wastelands. Their path was marked by the ghosts of the past - the remnants of a civilization that had been

consumed by fire, the echoes of a world that no longer existed.

They scavenged for supplies, hunted for food, and fought off mutated creatures, each day a desperate struggle for survival.

They found solace in each other, their bonds forged in the crucible of hardship, their shared experiences a language of resilience and defiance.

With each step forward, Lila's past haunted her, the memories of her brother's death a constant shadow. She wrestled with the guilt of survival, questioning whether she was worthy of continuing in a world that had stolen everything from her. But the embers of hope kept flickering, a beacon of light guiding her through the darkness.

As they ventured deeper into the ruins, they encountered remnants of the old world, decaying monuments to a bygone era. They discovered hidden bunkers, abandoned research facilities, and forgotten archives, each offering a glimpse into the secrets of the past. These clues were like pieces of a shattered puzzle, leading them closer to the truth, but each revelation came at a price.

The journey was testing their trust in each other, pushing them to their limits. The weight of responsibility pressed down on Ethan, forcing him to make difficult decisions.

Suspicion, like a venomous vine, began to creep through their ranks, threatening to unravel the fragile bonds that held them together.

Lila, with her sharp mind and unwavering determination, became the group's strategist, their anchor in the storm. She navigated treacherous terrain, deciphered cryptic clues, and used her skills to protect her fellow survivors. But even her strength was tested, her resilience challenged as she grappled with the darkness that threatened to engulf her.

The journey was not just a quest for the truth, but a journey into the depths of human nature. They encountered other

groups of survivors, each operating with its own set of rules and beliefs. Some were driven by greed and power, others by desperation and fear.

Their encounters highlighted the harsh reality of the post-apocalyptic world - a world where survival meant bending or breaking the rules, a world where trust was a rare commodity and betrayal a constant threat. They faced moral dilemmas, forced to make choices that challenged their principles and tested their humanity.

In the face of adversity, Lila and the Echoes held on to their shared hope. They were a testament to the resilience of the human spirit, a beacon of light in a world consumed by darkness. Their journey was a testament to the indomitable spirit of those who dared to hope for a better future, to fight for a world that had been lost, and to embrace the power of human connection in the face of unimaginable hardship.

Haunted by Memories

Chapter 2: Scars of the Past

The desolate landscape stretched before her, a canvas painted in shades of gray and brown. The wind, a constant companion in this wasteland, whipped at her face, carrying with it the scent of dust and decay. Lila shielded her eyes, the memory of the firestorm that had consumed her world still a searing scar on her mind. The image of her brother, his hand reaching out to her, a silent plea in his eyes, flashed before her. It was a vision she couldn't escape, a recurring

nightmare that haunted her every waking moment.

The guilt gnawed at her, a venomous serpent twisting in her gut. She had

survived, while he hadn't. Why? The question echoed in the empty spaces of her mind, a relentless tormentor. Was it a cruel twist of fate or a testament to her own innate resilience? She couldn't tell anymore. The line between her strength and her survival instincts had blurred, leaving her to grapple with the dark whispers of self-doubt.

The world had changed. It was a cold, unforgiving place, where trust was a fragile commodity and survival a daily struggle.

The apocalypse had stripped humanity of its illusions, exposing its raw, primal instincts. In this harsh reality, Lila had trans-formed into a scavenger, a ghost drifting through the remnants of a lost civilization. She had honed her skills, becoming adept at navigating the ruins, scavenging for scraps of food and supplies, and utilizing her knowledge of the pre-apocalyptic world to her advantage.

But even her hardened exterior couldn't fully shield her from the emotional turmoil that raged within. The memories of the past, like ghostly apparitions, emerged from the shadows, their icy fingers clutching at her heart. The screams of the innocent, the blinding flashes of light, the suffocating smoke, and the bone-chilling silence that followed – they were all etched into her mind, an indelible mark of the apocalypse's destructive power.

The guilt was a constant companion, a suffocating weight that threatened to crush her. It whispered in her ears, painting her survival as a betrayal, a dark stain on her soul. She had chosen to live while others had perished, a decision she couldn't shake.

The journey with the group offered a glimmer of hope, a fragile oasis in the desert of her despair. Their shared experiences, their struggles for survival, and their determination to uncover the truth had forged a fragile bond, a sense of

belonging that she had desperately craved. But the darkness within her was persistent, a constant reminder of the trauma that she had endured.

As they traversed the desolate landscapes, the weight of her memories became an oppressive burden. The ruins they passed, skeletal remnants of a forgotten world, triggered a torrent of emotions – grief, anger, and a profound sense of loss. Each shattered building, each abandoned car, whispered tales of a life that had been brutally cut short, mirroring the tragedy she had personally endured.

Lila knew that the past could not be undone, but its grip on her was relentless.

The darkness threatened to consume her, to drown her in a sea of self-loathing and despair. But she clung to the hope that her resilience, the very quality that had allowed her to survive, could also be the force that would help her overcome the demons that haunted her.

The journey was a test of her will, a constant battle against the memories that threatened to destroy her. She knew she had to find a way to reconcile with her past, to confront the guilt and the pain, and to move forward. The weight of survival was a heavy one, but it was a burden she had to carry, not just for herself, but for the future she longed to create.

The Scars of the Land

The rusty, skeletal remains of a once-thriving city stretched out before them, a graveyard of twisted metal and shattered glass. The wind, a constant companion in this desolate world, whipped around them, carrying the bitter tang of decay and the faint, acrid scent of ash. The landscape, once a vibrant tapestry of life, now resembled a canvas painted in shades of gray and brown, scarred by the fiery touch of the apocalypse.

Lila, her face hardened by the harsh realities of survival, stared out at the wreckage with a mixture of dread and a strange, perverse fascination. The city was a monument to the past, a reminder of what was lost and what could never be reclaimed. It was a constant reminder of the day the world ended, a day she couldn't erase from her memory, no matter how hard she tried.

Their journey had been fraught with peril. They had navigated through fields of mutated vegetation, their leaves sharp as knives and their roots as thick as tree trunks, a grotesque parody of nature. The twisted remains of once-familiar creatures stalked the shadows, their bodies warped and deformed by the radiation that permeated the air. Their eyes, burning with a chilling hunger, reflected the same darkness that seemed to consume the world around them.

They had scavenged for food and supplies in abandoned settlements, their interiors choked with dust and silence. The echo of the past lingered within these broken homes, whispering stories of families torn apart, of lives shattered and dreams extinguished. The remnants of normalcy - a child's toy, a tattered photograph, a half-finished meal - were

poignant reminders of the human cost of the apocalypse.

They had encountered other groups of survivors, their faces drawn and weary, their eyes wary. Some were desperate, clinging to the remnants of a civilization that had long crumbled. Others were hardened, their survival instincts sharpened into weapons, their hearts filled with suspicion and distrust. The world had become a battleground for resources, a constant struggle for survival, and the lines between friend and foe were often blurred.

Each day was a test of their strength, their resolve, and their faith in one another. They pushed on, driven by a shared desire for answers and a glimmer of hope that, despite the devastation, a future was possible. But the journey had taken its toll. The scars of the land mirrored the scars etched deep within their souls.

As they trudged through the desolate landscape, Lila felt a familiar pang of guilt. It was the guilt of survival, the burden of carrying on when so many others hadn't. She tried to push it down, bury it beneath layers of cynicism and self-

preservation, but it always found its way back to the surface, a persistent reminder of the life she had lost, the loved ones she had left behind.

The weight of the past pressed heavily on her, a suffocating cloak that threatened to consume her. She was haunted by the memory of her brother, his lifeless eyes staring back at her from the darkness of her nightmares. The guilt gnawed at her, a constant reminder of the choices she had made, the sacrifices she had been forced to make to survive.

But even as the darkness threatened to engulf her, Lila knew she couldn't succumb to it. She had to keep going, not just for herself, but for the others who relied on her strength and resilience. They had a purpose, a mission that transcended

their own personal struggles: to uncover the truth, to find out what had happened, and to fight for a future that seemed impossible.

As they continued their trek, their path leading them deeper into the ravaged heartland, Lila couldn't help but feel a sense of foreboding. The world was a cruel and unforgiving place, and the scars of the past ran deep, threatening to consume them all. Yet, she held onto the hope that somewhere amidst the ruins, there was still a flicker of light, a chance for

redemption, a path towards a new dawn. For if the world could be reborn from the ashes, so too could they.

The Trust Game

The journey into the desolate heartlands was a constant test of their mettle. Each day brought a new challenge, a new threat that gnawed at their dwindling reserves of hope. The land itself was a living testament to the apocalypse, its scars etched deep into the ravaged landscape. Twisted metal skeletons of once-proud buildings jutted out from the earth, their rusted forms a macabre reminder of a lost civilization.

The air hung heavy with the stench of decay and ash, a constant reminder of the tragedy that had befallen them.

The group had become a microcosm of the world they were navigating, their survival intertwined with the fragile threads of trust that held them together. As they ventured deeper into the wilderness, suspicion grew like a noxious weed, spreading its tendrils of doubt amongst them. Their shared ordeal had forged a bond of necessity, but the strain of constant danger and the weight of the unknown gnawed at their unity.

The burden of leadership fell heavily on Ethan, his weathered face etched with the weight of his responsibilities.

He was a man of action, a natural leader who had guided them through countless perils. But even his strength wavered beneath the weight of their shared anxieties. The scars of his past, the ghosts of choices made in a world gone mad, haunted him, creating a chasm of doubt that threatened to engulf him.

Lila, with her sharp wit and unwavering resolve, became a beacon of strength for the group. She had faced her own demons, the trauma of losing her brother burned deep within her, a constant reminder of the fragility of life. Yet, she

refused to surrender to the despair that threatened to

consume them all. Her sharp eyes scanned their

surroundings, always on the lookout for danger, her mind a whirlwind of strategies for survival. She knew that the true danger lay not only in the harsh realities of their post-

apocalyptic world, but also within the hearts of those she had come to trust.

The tension within the group was palpable. Whispers of discontent circulated like a virus, infecting their once-solid unity. A sense of unease permeated their interactions, every word spoken with a cautious reserve. Each challenge they faced, from scavenging for food to fending off mutated creatures, served only to amplify their suspicion. The shared struggle for survival, which had once brought them together, now became a crucible in which their trust was tested to its breaking point.

The whispers started with a single, innocuous question: who had betrayed them in the ruins of the city? The betrayal had left a deep scar, a raw wound that wouldn't heal. The culprit had vanished, leaving only a trail of unanswered questions and a gnawing sense of betrayal. Now, as they navigated the perilous landscape, the seeds of doubt were sown.

Every decision, every action was scrutinized. Their bond was fragile, each member holding onto the frayed threads of trust with a desperate grip. The weight of suspicion hung heavy in the air, a constant threat to unravel their fragile unity.

One evening, huddled around a flickering campfire, the tension reached a breaking point. Lila, with a weariness that went beyond the physical exhaustion of their journey, spoke up. Her voice, usually so confident, was now laced with a tremor of doubt.

"We need to talk. We can't keep going like this, all these

whispers, these suspicions. It's eating us from the inside."

Her words cut through the silence like a knife, piercing the fragile peace that had settled over the group.

The other survivors looked at each other, their expressions mirrored a mixture of fear and anxiety. Ethan, his face etched with concern, spoke up, his voice a deep rumble that echoed through the night.

"Lila's right. We can't let this fester. We need to address this, to find a way to move forward together."

His words were reassuring, but the underlying tension remained. The trust game, played out in the shadow of the apocalypse, was proving to be a dangerous game. Their fate, their survival, hinged on their ability to overcome the darkness that threatened to consume them. The future was uncertain, shrouded in the shadows of a world gone mad, but one thing was certain: the journey ahead would require an unwavering faith in each other, a faith that was rapidly dwindling beneath the weight of suspicion and fear.

Echoes of the Past

The air hung heavy with the scent of decay, a cloying reminder of the world that had been. The rusted remnants of a once bustling city stretched before Lila, a testament to the devastating power of the apocalypse. She navigated the labyrinthine maze of shattered buildings with practiced ease, her worn boots crunching on broken glass and crumbling concrete. The echoes of the past were everywhere, whispering secrets in the rustle of the wind and the groaning of the steel skeletons.

Lila's heart ached with a familiar, gnawing emptiness, a constant reminder of the life she had lost. The memory of her brother, his hand clenched around hers, his eyes wide with fear as the sky turned crimson, was a wound that refused to heal. She had survived, against all odds, but the price of survival was etched upon her soul, a dark stain that she couldn't scrub away.

Her fingers traced the worn leather of her satchel, a small treasure trove of salvaged items – a tattered map, a rusted compass, a cracked mirror that reflected a face weathered beyond its years. She was a survivor, a scavenger who had learned to adapt to the desolate landscape, finding solace in the rhythms of her solitary existence. She had honed her skills, learned to read the signs of the ravaged world, and mastered the art of extracting sustenance from the barren earth. But the solitude had its price. It had hardened her, carved a wall around her heart that she had built to protect herself from further pain.

Yet, the silence wasn't always peaceful. The city, a tomb of forgotten dreams, pulsed with a faint, unsettling rhythm, a

whisper of something hidden beneath the layers of decay.

She had felt it ever since the day she discovered the

message, scrawled on a scrap of parchment that seemed to have materialized from the dust. It spoke of a conspiracy, a truth concealed beneath the ashes of the world, a truth that could unravel everything she thought she knew.

It was a fragile piece of hope, a spark of defiance in the darkness. She had entrusted the message to the group, the only semblance of a family she had found since the world had ended. They were a ragtag band of survivors, each bearing the scars of the past in their eyes, yet driven by a shared desire for a future, a future that promised a world where they could reclaim their humanity.

But the journey had taken its toll. The scars of the land, the wounds of betrayal, the constant battle for survival had taken their toll. They had lost members, the whispers of grief mingling with the harsh cries of the wind. She had witnessed the darkness that lurked within each of them, the fragile line between hope and despair that could snap at any moment.

The message had become a shared beacon, a promise of answers, a way to break free from the cycle of pain. It had drawn them together, forged a fragile bond of trust in a world where trust was a luxury they could no longer afford.

They had traversed treacherous landscapes, navigated the ruins of the old world, and faced the monstrous echoes of the past that haunted their every step.

And yet, the message remained a riddle, a fragmented whisper that tantalized and frustrated in equal measure. Lila felt a familiar ache, a sense of being on the brink of understanding, a feeling she had known before the apocalypse, before her life had been torn apart. She had always been drawn to the mysteries, the hidden truths that lay beneath the surface of everyday existence. It had been

her downfall, her obsession with uncovering the secrets of the world that had led to the cataclysmic event. Now, in this ravaged world, she was once again seeking answers, driven by the same insatiable curiosity.

She found herself wandering through the skeletal frame of a library, the once vibrant repository of knowledge now a mausoleum of dusty tomes. She had spent days combing through the wreckage, a determined search for any shred of information that could lead her closer to the truth. And then, she found it, buried beneath a mountain of shattered shelves.

A single book, its cover worn and faded, its title a faded

whisper – "The Architect of Fate."

Her heart pounded against her ribs. This was it, the key she had been seeking. It was a historical text, detailing the rise and fall of a clandestine organization known as the Obsidian Society. It was a name she recognized, a name that had whispered in the depths of her nightmares ever since the apocalypse.

She flipped through the brittle pages, her eyes scanning the archaic script. She read of a group of brilliant minds, scientists, politicians, and strategists, who had manipulated the world from the shadows, their motives veiled in secrecy, their methods shrouded in ambiguity. They believed they were guiding humanity, molding it into a new world order, one where they were the architects of fate, the puppet masters of the world's destiny.

She read of a secret project, a weaponized virus engineered to cull the population, to reshape the world in their image. It was a chilling tale of ambition, greed, and the dark side of human nature. It was a story that mirrored the events of the apocalypse, the terrifying realization that the world had not ended by accident but by design.

The weight of the truth settled upon her, a crushing burden.

She had always known, in the darkest corners of her mind, that the apocalypse was not just a random event. There was something deeper, something more sinister at play. And now, she was facing the truth, a truth that was both terrifying and liberating.

Her fingers trembled, her breath catching in her throat. She read on, the words blurring as tears welled up in her eyes.

The Obsidian Society had infiltrated every level of government, manipulated the media, and used their influence

to control the world. And now, she was staring at the
blueprint of their destruction.

Lila closed the book, her mind reeling from the revelations.
She was not just a survivor; she was a witness, a bearer of a truth
that had the power to destroy the world she had come to know.
The Obsidian Society's plan had been thwarted, but their legacy
remained. She was determined to unravel the secrets of their
past, to expose their crimes to the world, and to ensure that
their madness would never again cast a
shadow over humanity.

She knew this was just the beginning. The path ahead was
shrouded in uncertainty, fraught with dangers both seen and
unseen. But the knowledge she had gained was a weapon, a
source of strength. She had faced the echoes of the past, and she
had emerged from the ruins stronger, more determined.

She was no longer just a survivor. She was a warrior, a
guardian of the truth, fighting for a future where humanity could
reclaim its destiny.

A New Enemy Emerges

The sun dipped below the horizon, casting long shadows
across the desolate landscape. The air, thick with dust and the
faint scent of decay, held a chilling stillness. The group had
been traveling for days, their journey marked by the constant
threat of danger and the gnawing hunger that gnawed at their
bellies. Lila, her eyes weary and her spirit strained, scanned the
horizon, her gaze searching for any sign of life, any hope that
could pierce through the
suffocating darkness that seemed to envelop them.

Their progress was slow and arduous. The remnants of the old
world, now twisted and decaying, presented obstacles at every

turn. Crumbling concrete structures, once symbols of human achievement, now served as deadly traps, their

jagged edges waiting to tear flesh and bone. Twisted metal, a testament to the fiery wrath of the apocalypse, lay scattered like broken toys, a constant reminder of the devastation that had consumed their world.

Ethan, the group's leader, his face weathered and hardened by the trials they had endured, kept a watchful eye on their surroundings. He was a man of few words, but his actions spoke volumes. He had a quiet strength about him, a sense of purpose that had drawn Lila and the others to him.

"Keep your eyes peeled, everyone," Ethan barked, his voice hoarse from the dry air. "We're not out of the woods yet."

The words echoed in the silence, a stark reminder of the vulnerability they faced. They were just a small band of survivors, clinging to the hope of a better tomorrow,

surrounded by a world that seemed to be conspiring against

them.

As the sun dipped below the horizon, they reached a fork in the road. They had been following the remnants of a long-abandoned highway, a trail that had led them through the heart of the wasteland. Now, the road split, each path

shrouded in shadows, promising both danger and the
possibility of discovery.

"We'll split up," Ethan announced, his voice firm. "Lila, you and Marcus take the left path. I'll go right with Sarah and Jacob. We'll meet up at the crossroads in two hours."

Lila hesitated for a moment. She trusted Ethan, but

something about the split felt wrong. She knew that their numbers were already small, and the thought of separating into even smaller groups made her uneasy.

"Are you sure about this, Ethan?" she asked, her voice laced with concern. "We're already stretched thin."

Ethan nodded, his gaze unwavering. "We need to cover more ground if we want to find what we're looking for. And besides, there's safety in numbers."

Lila didn't share his confidence, but she knew that arguing wouldn't change his mind. She and Marcus set off down the left path, their footsteps echoing in the silence, a sound that seemed to reverberate through the empty spaces of the ruined world.

The left path was just as treacherous as the highway they had been following. The road was littered with debris, making their progress slow and painstaking. The silence was broken only by the occasional screech of a crow overhead or the rustling of leaves in the sparse trees that lined the path.

Lila kept a sharp eye out for any sign of danger. She knew that the wasteland was teeming with threats – mutated creatures that lurked in the shadows, scavengers who preyed on the weak, and the unseen horrors that lay dormant in the ruins.

As they walked, Lila found herself lost in thought. She couldn't shake the feeling that they were being watched, that unseen eyes were following their every move. The weight of the past, the memories of the apocalypse and the loved ones she had lost, pressed down on her, threatening to crush her spirit.

"Are you alright, Lila?" Marcus asked, his voice laced with concern. He had been with the group since the beginning, a quiet and steady presence in the midst of chaos.

Lila forced a smile, hoping to reassure him. "I'm fine," she said, her voice betraying the tremor in her hands. "Just a little tired. You?"

"Same here," Marcus replied, his own face etched with fatigue. "This place... it's heavy. It weighs on you, even when you try to forget."

They walked in silence for a while, each lost in their own thoughts, their hearts filled with a shared sense of dread. The world around them, a canvas of broken dreams and shattered hopes, reflected the turmoil within them.

As the sun began to set, casting long shadows across the path, they heard a noise. It was a distant sound, barely audible, but it was enough to send a shiver down Lila's spine. She stopped, her eyes darting to the shadows that clung to the edges of the road.

"Do you hear that?" she whispered, her voice barely audible

above the rustle of the wind.

Marcus nodded, his eyes narrowed. "Sounds like something's moving. We need to be careful."

They pressed on, their senses heightened, their footsteps barely audible. The noise grew louder, a low rumble that seemed to shake the ground beneath their feet.

"It's getting closer," Marcus whispered, his voice laced with fear. "We need to find cover."

Lila scanned the landscape, her gaze searching for any sign of shelter. The path was narrow, surrounded by dense undergrowth, offering little protection from whatever was approaching.

Just ahead, they spotted a large, abandoned warehouse. The rusted steel doors stood open, revealing a cavernous interior that was shrouded in darkness. It wasn't the ideal place to take

34

cover, but it was their best option.

"We need to get inside," Lila said, her voice barely above a whisper. "Whatever that is, it's not going to wait for us."

They hurried towards the warehouse, their hearts pounding in their chests. As they reached the entrance, the noise intensified, the ground vibrating with the force of the approaching threat.

"It's not a creature," Marcus gasped, his eyes wide with fear. "It's... it's a vehicle."

Lila's heart sank. They had been warned about raiders, groups of survivors who preyed on the weak and the vulnerable. They were brutal, ruthless, and they would stop at nothing to get what they wanted.

They reached the warehouse, and Lila pushed open the rusted steel doors, the noise of the approaching vehicle momentarily drowned out by the groan of the metal. The interior was dark and dusty, the air thick with the smell of decay and neglect. They could hear the rhythmic thud of the approaching vehicle, growing louder with every passing moment.

They had only seconds to prepare. Lila grabbed a rusty pipe from a stack of debris near the entrance, her fingers tightening around its cold metal. Marcus reached for a discarded metal box, a heavy makeshift weapon in the absence of anything better.

The noise of the vehicle suddenly stopped. Silence descended, thick and heavy, broken only by the sound of their own ragged breathing.

"They're waiting," Marcus whispered, his voice trembling. "They're watching us."

The warehouse doors creaked open, and a shaft of light illuminated the dusty interior. The silhouette of a large truck, its headlights blinding in the darkness, stood at the entrance.

From the shadows, a group of figures emerged, their faces obscured by the darkness, their bodies clad in worn and ragged clothing.

"You're outnumbered," a gruff voice spoke from the shadows. "You're trapped."

The raiders, their faces hidden behind masks of dirt and desperation, circled them, their eyes glittering with a predatory hunger. The atmosphere was thick with tension, the air crackling with anticipation. Lila could feel her own pulse quickening, her heart pounding against her ribs.

They had stumbled into a trap, and the hunters were closing in. They were outnumbered, outgunned, and trapped in a warehouse with no escape. And the only thing standing between them and the raiders' hunger was the rusty pipe in her hand and the fear that gnawed at her heart.

They were not just fighting for their lives, they were fighting for the hope of a better future. They were fighting for the dream of a world where humanity could rebuild, a world where the horrors of the past could be overcome.

But as the raiders advanced, their faces masked by shadows, their intentions clear, Lila knew that they were facing an enemy far more dangerous than any creature that might lurk in the wasteland. This enemy was human. This enemy was driven by greed, by desperation, by the darkest instincts of survival.

And Lila, her heart heavy with the weight of their situation, knew that this was a battle they might not survive.

The Weight of Secrets

5

Chapter 3: The Crossroads

The wind howled through the skeletal remains of the city, carrying with it the scent of decay and the whisper of a past that refused to be silenced. Lila stood on the precipice of a decision that would shape the course of her life and the fate of those who had become her beacon of hope in this desolate world. The weight of secrets pressed down on her, a burden she had carried for too long.

She stared at the tattered map spread out before her, its faded lines tracing a route that promised both salvation and danger. The truth, the one she had stumbled upon, was a venomous serpent coiled around her heart, threatening to suffocate her. To reveal it, to expose the dark underbelly of the world they inhabited, would be a gamble. A gamble that could dismantle the fragile trust she had built with Ethan and the others, leaving them vulnerable and adrift in a sea of uncertainty.

It all began with the whispers, faint echoes from the past, carried by the wind that swept through the broken city. She had discovered a hidden bunker, its entrance obscured by rubble and time. Inside, dusty scrolls and faded documents whispered tales of a conspiracy so vast, so horrifying, that it seemed impossible.

The truth, concealed beneath layers of deceit and lies, spoke of a calculated apocalypse, a meticulously orchestrated act of betrayal that had plunged the world into chaos.

Ethan, the charismatic leader of the group, had been a beacon of hope, a symbol of strength in a world shattered by despair. But as Lila delved deeper into the abyss of her newfound knowledge, she began to question everything she had believed. His unwavering determination to uncover the truth felt fueled by something more, something that went beyond the collective desire for answers.

The truth had the potential to shatter their fragile unity, to sow seeds of doubt and mistrust that could tear them apart. Yet, the weight of her secrets pressed heavily on her conscience. To conceal it, to keep the truth locked within her, would be a betrayal of her own principles, a violation of the trust she had entrusted to those who had become her family in this desolate wasteland.

The memory of her brother, the last vestige of her former life, flashed through her mind, his warm smile a haunting reminder of what she had lost. He had always believed in her, encouraged her to fight for what was right, even when the world seemed to be collapsing around them. And now, she found herself at a crossroads, forced to make a choice that could redefine their destiny.

She closed her eyes, her heart pounding against her ribs like a trapped bird. Every fiber of her being screamed for her to protect the group, to shield them from the darkness that lurked in the shadows. But her soul yearned for justice, for the truth to be unveiled, no matter the cost.

Lila's past was etched upon her soul, a tapestry woven with threads of loss and grief. The apocalypse had stolen everything from her, leaving her with a void that gnawed at her insides. She had learned to survive, to adapt, to thrive in this desolate world, but the scars remained, a constant reminder of the life she had lost. The weight of those memories, the guilt of surviving when others had perished, burdened her every step.

She thought of the others, their faces etched in her memory. Maya, with her unwavering spirit and fierce determination, a shield against the storms of despair.

Jax, with his silent strength and unwavering loyalty, a pillar of support in their darkest moments. And Ethan, with his captivating aura and unyielding resolve, a leader who had inspired her to rise from the ashes of her past.

But there was a darkness within him, a flicker of something that sent chills down her spine. He spoke of the truth, of uncovering the secrets that had shattered their world. But there was a hint of something else in his eyes, a glimmer of ambition that made her uneasy.

Lila could feel the pressure building, the tension tightening around her like a noose. The crossroads before her was not just a geographical marker, but a symbolic divide between the life she had built and the one she was destined to lead. The truth, she knew, had a price. It was a price she was willing to pay, but she feared the toll it would take on those she had come to care for.

Her hands trembled as she reached for the tattered map, the lines blurring as her vision clouded with a mixture of fear and determination. She needed to speak, to reveal what she had discovered, but the fear of shattering the fragile trust they had built held her back.

The wind picked up, whistling through the skeletal remains of the city, a

mournful symphony that seemed to echo the turmoil raging within her. Lila knew that the choice she had to make was not just about her, but about them, about the future they were trying to build in the ashes of a world that had been lost.

She closed her eyes and took a deep breath, the weight of her decision pressing down on her. This was her moment of truth, the precipice where she had to choose between the burden of her secrets and the responsibility of revealing the

truth, no matter the consequences. The weight of the world, it seemed, rested on her shoulders, a responsibility she could not escape.

The Price of Survival

The air hung heavy with the weight of their decision. It had been a long night, filled with hushed whispers and tense exchanges. They had gathered around a flickering lantern, its feeble light struggling to pierce the gloom that had settled upon them like a shroud.

The discovery of the abandoned bunker had shaken them to their core. It was a relic of a forgotten time, a testament to the world that had been. But within its rusted walls, they had unearthed a chilling truth. It wasn't just a forgotten

storehouse of supplies; it was a repository of secrets. The government's dark agenda, hidden beneath layers of rust and dust, whispered of a calculated event, a deliberate act of destruction.

Their discovery had given them a glimpse into the abyss of human greed and manipulation, leaving them grappling with a new kind of horror. The world they thought had been lost to a catastrophic event was, in fact, a product of deliberate design. And now, the question loomed over them like a storm cloud, threatening to unleash its wrath upon their fragile hope.

"We can't just walk away from this," Alex, their gruff, yet kind-hearted leader, said, his voice echoing in the cavernous space. "We know the truth. We can't let it stay buried. We owe it to the people we lost, to the world that was, to find a way to expose this."

But the weight of responsibility pressed heavily upon them. Their journey had been fraught with danger. They had witnessed firsthand the brutality of the world they now

inhabited. The struggle for survival had forced them to make difficult choices, to compromise their morality in the face of desperation.

Lila, their resourceful scavenger, the one who had unearthed the truth, remained silent. Her heart was a battlefield of conflicting emotions. The memory of her brother's death, the chilling silence of the world after the bombs, had haunted her every waking moment. The truth had ripped open old wounds, exposing the raw nerve of grief and anger. She had always sought solace in the tangible, in the ability to find, to scavenge, to rebuild. But this discovery, this truth, was a weapon that threatened to tear them apart.

"We're not equipped for this," a young woman named Sarah whispered, her voice barely a murmur. "We're just trying to survive. We can't take on the government. We'll be crushed."

The others nodded in agreement. The weight of their own survival hung heavy in the air. They had already faced so much loss. They had been forced to abandon their humanity, their values, in order to survive.

"We can't just leave it," Lila said, her voice firm, but laced with a tremor. "What if they're still doing this? What if there are more bunkers like this, more secrets, more people waiting to be sacrificed?"

Lila's words struck a chord. The thought of others suffering, of the world being manipulated for the sake of power, ignited a spark of defiance within them. They had been survivors, not just for themselves, but for the hope that a better world could be built.

"We need to be smart about this," Alex said, his voice thoughtful. "We can't walk into their headquarters screaming about a conspiracy. They'll just kill us. We need a plan."

"What are our options?" Sarah asked, her eyes wide with apprehension.

Lila stepped forward, the weight of the world pressing down on her shoulders. "We need to reach other survivors," she said. "We need to tell them what we found. We need to build a resistance."

Their eyes met, a silent pact forged in the flickering lamplight. The consequences of their choice were clear, but the weight of the truth, the burden of responsibility, was too heavy to bear alone. They were not just survivors; they were now guardians of the truth, keepers of the flame of hope in a world drowning in despair.

The journey ahead would be perilous, fraught with danger, and littered with the ghosts of their past. But they would face it together, united by a shared purpose. They would fight for a future where the truth was not a weapon of destruction but a beacon of hope, a testament to the enduring spirit of humanity.

A Moment of Truth

The air hung heavy with the scent of decay and tension. We were huddled around a flickering fire, the flames casting long, dancing shadows that seemed to mock our

vulnerability. It had been days since we had found any decent supplies, and the gnawing hunger in our stomachs mirrored the unease that had settled upon our hearts.

Lila, the firelight reflecting in her eyes, spoke in a voice that was both quiet and resolute. "We're running out of time," she said, her gaze unwavering. "And I think it's time we

addressed the elephant in the room."

Everyone knew who she was talking about. Daniel, the quiet, brooding member of our group, had been acting strangely since we'd crossed the abandoned city. His eyes were always darting, his demeanor guarded, and his words were few and far between.

He flinched at her words, his hand instinctively reaching for the worn leather strap that held his hunting knife. "What are you talking about, Lila?" he asked, his voice gruff.

"I know what you did," she said, her voice gaining in strength. "The ambush, the stolen supplies. You were the one who set us back."

Daniel's face hardened, his jaw tightening. "I don't know what you're talking about."

"Don't play dumb with me, Daniel. I saw your face. I saw the glint of fear and greed in your eyes. You thought we were weak, that you could take what you wanted."

A low growl erupted from the shadows. It was Ethan, our leader, his face etched with a mixture of anger and suspicion.

"What's going on here?"

Lila turned to him, her voice steady. "Daniel was behind the ambush. He's been taking supplies, selling them on the black market."

A gasp rippled through the group. The truth, so easily whispered, so carefully hidden, was now hanging in the air like a thick fog.

"It's not true," Daniel shouted, his voice laced with desperation. "You're just trying to throw me under the bus."

"Why would I do that?" Lila challenged, her voice rising. "You're the one who betrayed our trust. You're the one who put us all at risk."

Daniel took a step forward, his eyes burning with anger.

"Don't you dare accuse me. You're the one who's always been suspicious. You're the one who doesn't trust anyone."

"I trust people, Daniel," Lila countered. "But I also know that survival is a hard game. And sometimes, people make choices that they regret later. And sometimes, those choices lead to betrayal."

A tense silence fell over the group. The fire crackled ominously, the flames dancing like the ghosts of our past.

The air thickened, the weight of suspicion and betrayal hanging heavy between us.

Ethan, his face now etched with concern, spoke, his voice calm but firm. "Daniel, we need to talk. This is getting out of hand."

Daniel, his eyes now filled with a mixture of anger and fear, turned to Ethan, his voice hoarse. "There's nothing to talk about. I'm innocent."

"That's for us to decide," Ethan said, his voice low but commanding.

Lila knew this wasn't about Daniel anymore. It was about us, about the fragile bond we had forged in this desolate world. It was about our ability to trust each other, to believe in each other, even when the darkness threatened to consume us.

As the flames flickered, casting long, dancing shadows, Lila knew that this was a moment of truth. A moment that would shape our journey, a moment that would determine whether we were strong enough to survive, not just the dangers of the wasteland, but also the darkness within ourselves.

The Power of Hope

The air hung heavy with the scent of ash and despair. The group huddled around a flickering fire, its warmth a meager comfort against the chilling wind that whipped through the skeletal remains of the once-proud city. Lila, her face etched with fatigue and a stubborn defiance, stared into the dancing flames, her thoughts a chaotic jumble of grief, anger, and a flickering ember of hope.

The events of the past few weeks had been a whirlwind of betrayals, near-death experiences, and agonizing losses. They had lost a member of their group to the relentless grip of the post-apocalyptic world, their trust shattered by the revelation of hidden agendas and the corrosive power of fear.

It felt like a constant struggle against the encroaching darkness, a fight against the insidious whispers that echoed through the desolate landscape, whispering of a world where hope was a luxury they could no longer afford.

Yet, as Lila watched the faces around her, etched with weariness but also a flicker of resilience, a spark of defiance ignited within her. They were broken, battered, but not defeated. They were survivors, forged in the crucible of tragedy, bound together by a shared hunger for truth and a desperate yearning for a future that wasn't consumed by the ashes of the past.

She saw it in the weary eyes of Ethan, the charismatic leader who bore the weight of responsibility for their survival. She saw it in the stoic determination of Kai, the skilled hunter who had lost everything but his loyalty to the group. She saw it in the quiet strength of Maya, the resourceful medic who held their fragile existence together with her unwavering

compassion. They had been through hell and back, yet they still clung to a glimmer of hope, a belief that amidst the ruins of civilization, a new dawn could emerge.

It was a fragile hope, flickering like a candle in the wind, threatened by the relentless storms of doubt and despair. But it was a hope they couldn't afford to let die. The truth they sought, the answers they desperately craved, held the key to their survival, to their understanding of the world they had been thrust into.

Lila's own past, a tapestry woven with threads of grief and loss, had been a heavy anchor dragging her down. But as she looked at the faces of her companions, a newfound purpose began to take root within her. She wouldn't let the darkness consume them, wouldn't let their shared hope be

extinguished. They had been robbed of their past, but they still had the power to shape their future. They had the power to rebuild, to find a way to thrive in a world that seemed determined to tear them apart.

Lila knew that the road ahead would be arduous, fraught with danger and uncertainty. But she also knew that they wouldn't face it alone. They had each other, a fragile bond forged in the fires of adversity. They had their shared hope, a flicker of

defiance in the face of despair. And most
importantly, they had the truth, the knowledge that the
apocalypse wasn't a random act of fate, but a deliberate act of
destruction. It was a truth that could set them free, a truth they
would fight for, no matter the cost.

Lila knew that the journey wouldn't be easy. There would be
setbacks, betrayals, and moments where their hope would be
tested to its breaking point. But she also knew that they would
endure, that they would find strength in their shared purpose.
They would fight for a future that was worth

fighting for, a future where humanity could rise from the ashes
and rebuild a world where hope could finally take root.

A New Destination

The weight of the information they had gleaned settled heavily
on Lila's shoulders. Each piece of evidence, each shattered
fragment of the past, had chipped away at their hope for a simple,
accidental apocalypse. Now, a new reality was dawning – one of
deliberate manipulation and
unimaginable darkness. They were no longer simply
searching for survival; they were on a quest to expose the
truth, to find those responsible for this orchestrated
catastrophe.

Ethan, the group's charismatic leader, sat hunched over a
crude map, his brow furrowed in concentration. "We need to
get to the old government archives," he finally declared, his
voice rasping with exhaustion. "The information we found – the
coded messages, the fragmented data – it all points to a facility
near the old capital. It's a long shot, but it's our best chance."

Lila, ever cautious, raised a hand. "Are you sure about this?

It's a dangerous journey, even for a group as seasoned as ours. And what if the archives are empty? What if we're chasing ghosts?"

Ethan met her gaze, his eyes hard with determination.

"We're not chasing ghosts, Lila. We're chasing the truth. The truth that will set us free from the lies that bind us. It's a chance to understand what happened, to know why the world ended."

A wave of unease washed over Lila. She felt a familiar tug of fear, a fear that gnawed at the edges of her hope. This journey, this search for answers, felt more like a journey into

the depths of her own anxieties. But she knew she couldn't turn back. Not now. Not when the weight of the truth was pressing down on them all.

Their journey took them through a desolate, unforgiving landscape. The remnants of the old world, once vibrant and full of life, were now eerie monuments to a lost civilization.

Twisted metal carcasses of cars lay scattered like broken toys, their windows reflecting the harsh sun like fractured mirrors. Buildings, once towering symbols of progress, were now skeletal husks, their walls crumbling and their windows gaping hollow eyes.

They had to navigate treacherous terrain, their progress hindered by the ravaged landscape. Jagged rock formations, once paths for explorers and travelers, were now treacherous barriers, demanding careful maneuvering. The air, thick with dust and ash, choked their lungs and clung to their skin, leaving a gritty residue that reminded them constantly of the devastation that surrounded them.

As they trudged through this wasteland, the group began to feel the strain of their shared burden. The weight of the past, of

49

their collective loss and the constant threat of danger, began to chip away at their unity.

"How much longer?" Ben, the youngest of the group, asked one evening, his voice strained. He had been a cheerful presence, his youthful energy providing a flicker of lightness amidst the grim reality. Now, his youthful optimism seemed to have faded, replaced by a weary resignation.

Lila, sensing his distress, placed a hand on his shoulder. "We're getting closer," she said, forcing a reassuring smile. "Every mile we cover brings us closer to the truth. We have to keep moving forward. We owe it to ourselves."

Despite her words, even Lila couldn't shake the sense of foreboding that settled upon them like a shroud. The journey had become a crucible, testing their resolve and exposing the vulnerabilities within their fragile alliance.

One night, as they huddled around a crackling fire, their faces illuminated by the flickering flames, a sense of unease descended upon them. The wind, howling like a mournful cry, seemed to carry the weight of their shared fears. The silence between them was filled with unspoken anxieties, a stark reminder of the dangers that lurked in the shadows.

"We're being watched," Marcus, the group's skilled tracker, declared, his voice taut with tension. "I've seen tracks that shouldn't be here – human tracks, but not like ours. They're different, more... primal."

A chill snaked down Lila's spine. The news brought a new dimension of danger to their already precarious situation. They were not alone in this desolate world. Others were out there, and they weren't necessarily friendly.

Ethan, his eyes narrowed in suspicion, nodded in agreement. "Marcus is right. We need to be more vigilant. We're entering enemy territory."

The atmosphere crackled with tension, the shadows dancing around them like lurking figures. The once familiar sounds of the night – the rustle of leaves, the hooting of owls, the distant howl of a wolf – now sounded like whispers of warning, a symphony of unease.

As the sun began its slow descent, painting the sky in hues of orange and purple, they decided to move camp. The feeling of being watched, of being hunted, was too unsettling. The weight of the unknown pressed down on them, turning their once fragile hope into a fragile ember that could easily be

extinguished.

As they packed their meager belongings, Lila caught a glimpse of herself reflected in a chipped metal plate. Her reflection stared back at her, a ghost of her former self. The exhaustion etched onto her face, the hollowness in her eyes, were a grim testament to the hardships she had endured. But there was something else in her eyes, something that refused to be extinguished – a flicker of determination, a stubborn refusal to succumb to despair.

She knew this journey was far from over. The weight of the past, the ever-present threat of danger, and the unsettling knowledge of a conspiracy far more sinister than they could have imagined, were just the beginning. But she was

determined to see it through. The quest for truth, the fight for survival, and the desire to create a better world – these were the forces that fueled her.

They set off again, leaving the dying embers of the fire to fade into the darkness. As they walked, the desolate landscape stretched before them, a vast canvas of despair. But in the depths of that despair, Lila knew that they would find their strength. They had come too far, they had lost too much, to let the darkness consume them.

They were not just survivors; they were the last remnants of a broken world, determined to fight for a future that was still within their grasp. They were the last dawn, a flickering beacon of hope in a world consumed by shadows.

Haunted by the Past

Chapter 4: The Shadows of Doubt

The air hung heavy with the scent of decay and dust, a constant reminder of the world that had been. Ethan sat on a crumbling stone bench, his back to the remnants of a once-grand fountain, now choked with weeds and debris. The weight of the world pressed down on his shoulders, a familiar burden he'd carried for too long. He stared at the cracked concrete, the lines mirroring the fissures that ran deep within him.

The memories of his past life, the life before the bombs fell, rose like phantoms, their whispers echoing in the silence of the desolate landscape. He was a man who had once held a position of power, a man who had made choices he now regretted, choices that had shaped the world he now inhabited.

The apocalypse had been a turning point, a brutal awakening that had stripped him bare. It had forced him to confront the darkness within, the consequences of his actions. He'd seen the world burn, felt the despair of countless lives extinguished, and he carried the guilt of those he couldn't save.

Lila's words, "The apocalypse wasn't a natural disaster, it

was a calculated event," had struck a chord within him. It was a truth he'd known in the darkest corners of his soul, a truth he had fought to suppress. The revelation had ignited a flicker of hope, a chance to atone for the sins of the past, to bring justice to the world he had helped destroy.

He'd embraced the mantle of leadership, forming a band of survivors, their shared desperation binding them together. Yet, the past continued to haunt him.

The whispers of doubt, the fear of losing himself to the shadows of his past, weighed heavy on his heart.

"Ethan?" Lila's voice broke the silence, her concern evident in the gentle tone. She sat beside him, her eyes filled with a depth of understanding that touched him.

"I'm fine," he said, forcing a smile, his voice hollow. But Lila knew better. She knew the darkness that lurked within him, the demons that haunted his dreams.

"It's okay to talk about it," she said, her hand gently resting on his arm, a gesture of quiet comfort. "We're all burdened by the past, Ethan. We're all trying to find

a way to move forward."

Ethan met her gaze, his heart heavy with the weight of his secrets. He had made promises to himself, promises to the group, but he knew the truth. He was no hero, just a man struggling with the ghosts of his past, a man trying to find redemption in a world where hope was a fragile flame.

He took a deep breath, the scent of dust and decay filling his lungs, a constant reminder of the world he had helped to create.

"We have to be careful," he said, his voice low and tense. "We can't afford to trust anyone blindly." The weight of his words hung in the air, a shadow of doubt that threatened to consume them all.

The group had come so far, their journey riddled with danger and betrayal, yet they still had so much to face. The search for the truth behind the apocalypse had become their purpose, their only reason to keep fighting in a world on the brink of despair. But as they moved forward, the shadows of doubt loomed, a constant reminder that the past was never truly gone, that the darkness within could consume them all.

The journey would be long, filled with challenges, and Ethan knew he would have to confront his own demons, face the truth of his past, if he wanted to lead them to a brighter future. He had to learn to trust again, to find solace in the bonds they had forged, to embrace the strength they found in their shared struggle for survival.

Ethan's eyes met Lila's, their gazes locking in a silent exchange. They had a long road ahead, a road paved with the echoes of a shattered world, a road where the past haunted the present, and the future remained uncertain. They needed each other, their strengths and vulnerabilities intertwined, their hopes and fears woven into the fabric of their shared destiny.

But even in the face of the overwhelming darkness, they held onto a flicker of hope, a belief that the truth could set them free, that they could rise from the ashes of the old world and build a new dawn, a world where the shadows of doubt could finally be vanquished.

The Enemy Within

The sun beat down on their backs, turning the dusty trail ahead into a shimmering mirage. The air hung heavy with the scent of decay and the acrid tang of smoke, a constant reminder of the world they had lost. Lila wiped the sweat from her brow, her gaze fixed on the horizon, where the ruins of a long-forgotten city lay shrouded in a haze of dust. They had been traveling for days, their supplies dwindling, their spirits weary.

A sense of unease had settled over the group since their encounter with the raiders. The chilling brutality of their methods had shaken them to their core, a stark reminder of the depths of human depravity that could emerge in a world stripped bare.

Ethan, ever the stoic leader, had tried to maintain a facade of calm, but Lila sensed the turmoil beneath his controlled exterior. He had grown quiet, his gaze haunted by an unseen darkness. The raid had stirred up memories, she knew,

memories he desperately tried to suppress, but which now threatened to consume him.

As they approached the city, a wall of buildings towering over the desolate landscape, a wave of exhaustion swept over Lila. She could feel the weight of their journey pressing down on her, the burden of their shared past and their

uncertain future.

"We need to rest," she said, her voice rough with fatigue.

"We're not far from the settlement," Ethan replied, his voice lacking its usual vibrancy. "We should be able to find shelter

there."

Lila knew he was trying to be reassuring, but she couldn't shake the sense of foreboding that had taken root within her.

The settlement, a haven for survivors, was shrouded in mystery. Rumors had circulated among those they had encountered on their journey - stories of a place governed by harsh rules and a ruthless leader.

"What do we know about them?" she asked, her voice barely

a whisper.

Ethan hesitated, a flicker of unease crossing his face. "We've heard stories, whispers, but nothing concrete. We need to find out more."

As they pressed onward, the city loomed larger, its broken buildings casting long shadows across the scorched earth. They found a path through the rubble, navigating a maze of crumbling walls and twisted metal, their senses on high alert.

"They are there," Ethan said, his voice low and tense. "We need to be cautious."

He had spotted a faint glimmer of light ahead, a beacon of hope in the desolate landscape. As they approached, they saw a makeshift barricade, guarded by armed figures, their faces hidden by the shadows.

The air crackled with tension, a palpable sense of danger hanging heavy in the air. Ethan stepped forward, raising his hands in a gesture of peace. "We come in peace," he said, his voice firm but laced with a tremor of fear.

The figures remained silent, their eyes narrowed in suspicion. A moment stretched into an eternity, the silence broken only by the rustle of the wind through the ruins.

"We are seeking shelter," Ethan continued, his voice calm despite the pounding of his heart. "We are weary travelers."

One of the figures stepped forward, his gaze scanning them with a cold intensity. "We don't trust outsiders," he said, his voice gruff and unforgiving.

"We mean no harm," Ethan replied, his voice strained. "We simply need a place to rest."

The figure scrutinized them, his eyes lingering on Lila's worn clothes and her wary expression. He gestured for them to approach, his weapon still held at the ready.

As they crossed the barricade, Lila could feel the eyes of the other figures tracking their every move. Their faces were etched with suspicion, their postures tense with a coiled aggression that sent shivers down her spine.

"Welcome to the Sanctuary," the figure said, his voice lacking any warmth. "But be warned, this is a place of order, and those who break the rules will pay the price."

They were ushered into a courtyard, the heart of the settlement, a strange mix of ramshackle buildings and makeshift structures. People moved about, their faces etched with weariness, their eyes watchful.

A palpable sense of tension hung in the air, a silent acknowledgment of the precariousness of their existence.

Lila could sense the fear beneath the surface, a fear that simmered just below the surface, threatening to boil over at any moment. She felt a prickle of unease, a premonition of danger lurking in the shadows.

"This is our home," the figure said, his voice laced with a chilling pride. "We have built a place of safety, a place of order, in this chaotic world. Here, we are strong, here we are united, here we survive."

Lila looked around, her eyes taking in the faces around her. The women, hardened by hardship, their faces bearing the scars of survival. The men, their eyes filled with a steely determination, their hands calloused from years of toil.

The children, their innocence tainted by the world they had known, their eyes mirroring the bleakness of their existence.

They were survivors, yes, but they were also a reflection of the darkness that had taken hold in this shattered world.

The Enemy Within, a silent, insidious threat that had begun to seep into their hearts. It was a threat they could not see, could not touch, but which lingered in the shadows,

threatening to consume them all.

As they were led to a makeshift shelter, a dilapidated

building hastily repaired, Lila felt a sense of dread settle over her. They were safe, for now, but the shadows of doubt had begun to lengthen, casting a chilling light on the road ahead.

She couldn't shake the feeling that they had stumbled into a place where the fight for survival had become a twisted game, a descent into a world where morality had been sacrificed at the altar of self-preservation.

The Enemy Within, a dark reflection of the horrors they had faced, had taken root in this place. And Lila knew, with a cold dread, that this was just the beginning.

The Weight of Leadership

The weight of leadership sat heavy on Ethan's shoulders. It was a burden he hadn't anticipated, a responsibility that had snuck up on him like a shadow in the desolate landscape. Before the apocalypse, his life had been a series of impulsive choices, driven by a thirst for adventure and a disregard for consequences. Now, with the remnants of civilization

crumbling around them, every decision held the potential for life or death, for hope or despair.

The group relied on him. They looked to him for direction, for strength, for a semblance of order in a world that had been shattered. They saw in him a leader, a protector, a beacon of hope in the darkness. But the truth was, Ethan was as lost as they were, still grappling with the ghosts of his past, still haunted by the choices that had led him to this desolate existence.

The burden of their trust, the weight of their hopes, pressed down on him. He felt the pressure of their expectations, the scrutiny in their eyes, the silent questions that hung in the air.

Was he truly the leader they needed? Or was he just a man trying to make sense of a world that had gone mad?

His own doubts gnawed at him, whispering insidious

questions in the darkest corners of his mind. Was he leading them towards a better future, or was he simply delaying the inevitable? Was he guiding them toward a solution, or was he leading them towards a dead end? Each day, he faced a barrage of decisions, each one carrying the weight of their lives in its balance.

Lila, ever observant, had begun to notice the strain on Ethan.

She saw the flickering anxiety in his eyes, the weariness in his shoulders, the way he often retreated into silence, lost in his own thoughts. It was a far cry from the confident,

charismatic leader she had first encountered.

One evening, as they huddled around a flickering fire, she finally voiced her concerns. "Ethan," she said, her voice soft but firm, "You've been carrying a lot on your shoulders.

What's going on?"

Ethan hesitated, avoiding her gaze. He was a man of action, not of words, and the weight of his thoughts felt suffocating.

He wanted to confide in Lila, to share the burden of his doubts, but the fear of appearing weak, of shattering the image he had built, kept him silent.

He took a deep breath, forcing himself to meet her eyes. "It's just... I don't know if I'm the right person for this," he

confessed. "I'm not the same man I was before. I'm not sure I have the answers anymore."

Lila's expression softened. She understood the burden of his past, the weight of the choices he had made, the lingering regrets that shadowed his every step. "No one expects you to have all the answers, Ethan," she said gently. "We're all struggling to find our way in this new world. You're not alone."

Her words, simple yet powerful, offered him a glimmer of solace. It was a reminder that he was not alone in his

struggles, that his team, his comrades, shared in his burden.

They were all bound together by their shared past, their collective desire for a better future, and the unwavering belief that they could overcome the darkness that threatened to consume them.

That night, as they huddled around the fire, a sense of shared

vulnerability descended upon the group. They spoke openly about their fears, their doubts, their hopes. The weight of their individual burdens seemed to lighten, shared under the watchful gaze of the stars. They were a team, not a collection of individuals, and the strength of their unity was a testament to their resilience.

But the seeds of doubt had already been sown. Lila's

observation of Ethan's inner turmoil, coupled with his own confession, had opened a new chapter in the story. The shadows of doubt now loomed over their journey, a subtle but persistent presence that threatened to undermine their fragile unity.

The group's path forward was still shrouded in uncertainty.

They were navigating uncharted territory, facing unseen dangers, and grappling with the dark side of human nature. The weight of leadership, the burden of trust, and the ever-present threat of betrayal all conspired to cast a long shadow over their quest for truth and survival. Yet, despite the darkness, a flicker of hope remained. The shared belief in a better future, the unwavering determination to fight for a world free from the manipulation of the past, and the

enduring bonds of trust, fragile as they were, served as a beacon, guiding them through the shadows towards a new dawn.

The Seeds of Doubt

The days that followed were a slow burn of unease. Ethan, our leader, remained a steadfast figure, his strength a

reassuring presence amidst the uncertainty. Yet, Lila couldn't shake the feeling that something was amiss. Ethan's gaze, once filled with unwavering resolve, now seemed to flicker with a hidden agenda. He was distant, his mind occupied with thoughts he wouldn't share, his voice a monotone drone during our nightly fireside gatherings.

It started with small observations, fleeting moments that pricked at Lila's intuition. Ethan's meticulous planning, once a source of comfort, now felt like a veiled manipulation. His decisions, though seemingly for the collective good, carried an undercurrent of self-preservation that chilled Lila to the bone.

Then came the whispers, hushed conversations overheard in the dead of night. Whispers about Ethan's past, about the choices he made before the apocalypse, choices that had stained his soul. He had mentioned a "mistake" in the past, a cryptic remark that haunted Lila's dreams. What mistake could have been so profound, so unforgivable, as to merit a life lived in perpetual regret?

The seeds of doubt sprouted in fertile ground. The harsh realities of our post-apocalyptic existence, the constant threat of danger, had eroded our trust in each other. Every decision, every action, was scrutinized, weighed against the survival instincts that had become our guiding principles.

One evening, as we sat around the campfire, a chilling tale unfolded. A group of scavengers, desperate for resources,

had resorted to brutal tactics, preying on weaker settlements. Their methods were cruel and merciless, a stark reminder of the dark side of human nature that the apocalypse had

unleashed. The story left a heavy silence hanging in the air, the embers of the fire casting long, ominous shadows.

"They're no different from the raiders," Ethan remarked, his voice devoid of emotion.

But something in his tone, a subtle shift in his demeanor, caught Lila's attention. It wasn't the usual stoic Ethan, the man who had rallied us with his unwavering resolve. It was as if a mask had slipped, revealing a flicker of something else, something darker.

Lila dared to question him. "You think we're better than them?" she asked, her voice barely a whisper.

The firelight danced in Ethan's eyes, a strange intensity replacing the usual stoicism. He didn't answer immediately, his gaze fixed on the flames. "We have a purpose," he finally said, his voice low and gravelly. "We're not just scavenging. We're searching for something, something that will help us rebuild."

But Lila wasn't convinced. "And what if that purpose is not what it seems?" she pressed, her voice gaining a hint of defiance.

His gaze snapped up, meeting hers with a chilling intensity. "Don't question me, Lila," he said, his voice a warning. "We're all in this together. We need to trust each other."

That night, Lila couldn't sleep. Ethan's words echoed in her ears, fueling the growing doubt that gnawed at her. She knew he was hiding something, something he wasn't willing to share.

The next morning, as the sun cast a pale glow over the ruins, Lila approached the others, a heavy weight settling on her shoulders. She couldn't ignore the gnawing suspicion that something was amiss, that Ethan's leadership was not as pure as it appeared.

"There's something I need to tell you," Lila said, her voice hushed. "I think Ethan is not being honest with us. I think he's keeping secrets."

The others exchanged uneasy glances, the seeds of doubt that Lila had sown taking root. Had they been wrong to put their trust in Ethan? Was their leader truly guiding them towards a brighter future, or was he leading them down a path of darkness and deceit?

The air thickened with tension, the whispers of doubt now morphing into a chorus of fear and uncertainty. Lila, the scavenger who had always thrived on her independence, had become a catalyst for a reckoning within the group, a

reckoning that would reshape their fate and determine their survival in this brutal new world.

A Moment of Truth

The air hung thick with tension, the only sound the crackling of the dying fire. Lila sat across from Ethan, the flames reflecting in his deep-set eyes. They were both exhausted, their bodies worn down by the journey and the weight of the secrets they carried. Yet, the silence that had fallen between them was heavy with unspoken words, a simmering cauldron of doubt that threatened to boil over.

Lila had spent days wrestling with her suspicions, each piece of evidence she unearthed feeding the fire of her growing unease. Ethan, the charismatic leader, the man who had offered them hope in a world consumed by despair, seemed to be hiding something. His carefully crafted facade, the reassuring smile, the comforting words, felt like a mask now, a veil concealing a truth she desperately needed to know.

"Ethan, I have to talk to you," Lila's voice was quiet, a stark contrast to the turmoil churning within her.

Ethan's gaze hardened, his expression shifting from warmth to a guarded distance. "About what, Lila?"

"About what you're hiding."

The words hung in the air, a stark accusation that broke the fragile truce they had maintained. Ethan's silence stretched, the flames licking at the log with an unnerving intensity.

"I don't know what you're talking about," he said, his voice strained. "There's nothing I'm hiding."

Lila shook her head, a wave of frustration washing over her.

"That's not true. I've seen the way you look at me sometimes, the way you avoid my eyes. There's something you're not telling us, something you think you're protecting us from."

"You're letting your paranoia get the best of you," Ethan countered, his voice now laced with anger. "This is a hard life, Lila. It's easy to jump to conclusions, to see shadows where there are none."

"But you're not telling us the whole story, are you?" Lila persisted, her voice unwavering. "You've got secrets, Ethan. Secrets that could be dangerous, secrets that could destroy everything we've built together."

"Lila, enough!" Ethan's voice cracked with raw emotion. "You're making this harder than it has to be."

"No, Ethan, you are!" Lila's voice rose, the years of pent-up frustration finally bursting forth. "You're the one who's making this difficult. You're the one who's keeping us in the dark."

"You don't understand," Ethan said, his voice softening, a flicker of vulnerability breaking through his facade. "I'm doing what I have to do. I'm protecting us. You have to trust me, Lila."

"Trust?" Lila scoffed, a bitter laugh escaping her lips. "Trust is a luxury we can't afford anymore. We've been through too much, Ethan. We've seen the worst of humanity. You can't expect me to just blindly follow you anymore."

"Lila, listen to me..."

"No, Ethan, I'm done listening. I'm done with your secrets, your lies, your hidden agendas. I'm done being your pawn."

Their words hung in the air, charged with raw emotion, a testament to the cracks that were beginning to appear in the facade of their fragile unity. The flames danced, their flickering light casting grotesque shadows that seemed to mock the crumbling foundation of their trust.

Lila stood, her eyes fixed on Ethan, her voice a low growl, "Tell me the truth, Ethan. Tell me what you're hiding. Or we're done."

The silence that followed was deafening, punctuated only by the crackling of the dying fire. Ethan stared back at her, his face a mask of conflicted emotions. His silence, however, spoke volumes. He had nothing to say. Or perhaps, he had too much to say.

Lila turned and walked away, the weight of the truth, and the burden of the doubt, heavy on her shoulders. The journey ahead, she knew, would be far more perilous than she had ever imagined. The shadows of doubt had consumed them, and it was only a matter of time before they tore apart the fragile fabric of their hope.

The Price of Deception

7

Chapter 5: The Shifting Sands of Trust

Lila's heart pounded in her chest, a drumbeat of fear and betrayal. She had been wrong about Ethan, so very wrong. The man she had trusted, the man who had offered her a lifeline in the desolate world, had been hiding a secret, a truth that shattered the foundation of their fragile alliance.

It had started subtly, a fleeting glance, a whispered conversation overheard in the dim shadows of their makeshift camp. At first, Lila dismissed it as paranoia, a byproduct of living in a world where trust was a rare commodity. But the whispers grew louder, the glances more pointed. It became impossible to ignore the undeniable truth: Ethan was keeping something from them.

Driven by a mix of anger and desperation, Lila confronted him, her voice shaking with barely suppressed rage. "What are you hiding, Ethan? What is it about you that you can't tell us?"

Ethan's face, usually filled with a calm confidence, hardened into a mask of defiance. "There's nothing to hide, Lila. You're imagining things."

Lila's eyes narrowed, not believing a word. She had seen

the way he looked at them, the flicker of something cold and calculating in his eyes. He wasn't just hiding a secret, he was protecting something, someone.

The truth emerged in a slow, agonizing trickle. Ethan had been part of a small, secretive faction that had survived the apocalypse, a group that had thrived while others perished. They had a hidden base, a stockpile of resources, and a network of contacts that spanned the ruined landscape. It was a world of privilege and power, a world Lila could barely comprehend.

And Ethan, the man she had thought was a beacon of hope, had been a

participant in this secret society. He had chosen to leave his fellow survivors to their fate, to prosper while others struggled.

The news hit Lila like a physical blow. It was a betrayal of a magnitude she had never imagined. How could she, someone who had lost everything to the apocalypse, have been so naive?

The truth, once revealed, spread like wildfire, tearing through the group like a venomous serpent. Anger, suspicion, and fear festered in their hearts. The unity they had fought so hard to maintain crumbled, replaced by a bitter sense of disillusion-ment.

Lila watched as her fellow survivors turned on each other, their voices filled with venom and recriminations. The fragile bond that had kept them alive, that had offered a glimmer of hope in a world of despair, had been shattered.

Her heart ached with the pain of betrayal, but also with a burning sense of injustice. She couldn't let Ethan get away with this. She couldn't let his lies and manipulations remain unchecked.

With a steely resolve, Lila made a decision. She would leave

Ethan and his group behind. She would find her own way, a path that led not towards the comfortable world Ethan offered, but towards a future based on truth and justice.

Lila knew that the road ahead would be treacherous, filled with dangers both visible and unseen. But she was no longer the same vulnerable scavenger who had stumbled through the ruins of the old world. She had seen the darkness within humanity, the depths of betrayal, and the fragility of trust.

But she had also seen glimpses of hope, flickering flames of kindness and courage in the face of despair. She had witnessed the unwavering resilience of those who refused to give up, those who dared to dream of a better future.

Lila gathered her meager belongings, her gaze hardening with determination. She would seek the truth, even if it meant walking alone into the heart of darkness. She would find those responsible for the apocalypse, and she would hold them accountable for their actions. She would fight for a world where betrayal was a thing of the past, a world where the truth, no matter how painful, could finally prevail.

The Fallout

The air hung thick with a tension that threatened to suffocate them all. The campfire, once a comforting beacon in the bleak landscape, now flickered with a dying light, mirroring the waning hope in their hearts. The betrayal hung heavy, a stench of sulfur in the air. Ethan, the charismatic leader they once trusted, had lied. He'd kept secrets, cloaked in a veil of self-preservation, leaving them vulnerable and raw.

Lila's heart throbbed with a mixture of anger and disillusionment. The weight of Ethan's deception felt like a leaden fist crushing her chest. She'd seen the flicker of fear in his eyes, the way he'd retreated into a shell of defensive silence, a stark contrast to the confident leader he'd once been.

"I thought we were all in this together," Liam said, his voice laced with bitterness. He'd been the first to break the silence, his words like shards of glass piercing the fragile peace. "I thought we were fighting for something bigger than ourselves."

Lila found herself echoing Liam's sentiments. She'd clung to the hope that this group, this fragile alliance, was their salvation. It was a lifeline in a world where trust was a luxury they couldn't afford. Now, the very foundations of that hope were crumbling around them.

"We all have our secrets," Ethan mumbled, his gaze fixed on the dying embers. His words were a feeble attempt to justify his actions, but they fell flat, devoid of the power he once wielded. The weight of his deception had stripped him of his authority.

One by one, the other survivors spoke, their voices tinged with disappointment and resentment. They'd put their faith in Ethan, blindly following his leadership. Now, the realization that they'd been betrayed cut deep.

Lila saw the fear and uncertainty in the eyes of the others. They were adrift, their fragile sense of community shattered. The post-apocalyptic world was a harsh, unforgiving place, and now, the threat wasn't just from the elements or mutated creatures, but from each other.

She knew she couldn't stay. Staying would be a constant reminder of the betrayal, a constant struggle against the poison of doubt that had seeped into her heart. She needed to regain her footing, to find her own path, even if it meant walking away from the only semblance of family she'd found in this shattered world.

"I'm leaving," Lila said, her voice firm despite the tremor that ran through her. She could see the shock and surprise on their faces. They were caught between their anger at Ethan and their desire to hold on to the fragile remnants of their bond.

"Where will you go?" Liam asked, his voice heavy with concern.

"I'm going to find my own answers," Lila replied, her gaze unflinching. "I'm going to find the truth." She turned away, her heart heavy with the weight of betrayal and the uncertainty of the road ahead.

As she walked away, she glanced back at the group, at their faces etched with disappointment and a flicker of hope. Lila knew that she wasn't the only one who felt betrayed. The truth, like a wildfire, had consumed their trust, leaving

behind a smoldering wasteland.

The journey ahead would be solitary, perilous, and filled with uncertainty. But Lila knew that the truth was worth fighting for, even if it meant facing the darkness alone. The shifting sands of trust had betrayed her, but her determination to uncover the truth would remain steadfast. She would find her own answers, forge her own path, and embrace the perilous journey that lay ahead. The weight of the world, and the burden of truth, lay heavy on her shoulders, but she would bear it, for the sake of the future.

The Search for Truth

The sting of betrayal was still raw, a gaping wound in Lila's chest. She had been foolish, allowing Ethan's charisma to blind her to the cracks in his facade. Now, the group had fractured, splintered by suspicion and the bitter taste of deception.

Lila stood alone, watching the remnants of Ethan's group disappear into the dust-choked horizon. The weight of her choices pressed down on her, a crushing burden. Should she have stayed with them, clinging to the fragile hope of unity, or was this the only way forward? The truth, the need for justice, had called to her, drawing her towards a path fraught with uncertainty.

It was a gamble, a leap of faith into the unknown. But Lila couldn't bear the thought of living in a world where truth was buried beneath layers of lies and manipulation. She needed answers, not just for herself, but for the millions lost in the ashes of the old world.

She wasn't alone in her quest. A small group of survivors, their faces etched with hardship and determination, had gathered around her, drawn together by a shared yearning for justice. They were the ones who had never truly trusted Ethan, who had seen the flicker of darkness in his eyes even as the others clung to his promises.

Their names were whispers on the wind: Anya, a skilled tracker with eyes that held the wisdom of years spent navigating the desolate landscape; Kai, a young man whose nimble fingers could dismantle any lock and whose quiet strength spoke volumes; and Elias, a wizened old man who

carried the weight of the past on his shoulders, his memories of the pre-apocalyptic world a source of both sorrow and strength.

They formed an alliance, their bond forged in the fires of shared suffering and the unwavering hope for a better future.

Their journey was a testament to the enduring power of human connection, a beacon of light amidst the darkness. They would seek the truth together, their paths intertwined, their destinies intertwined.

Their first stop was a dusty, forgotten library, tucked away in the ruins of a once-thriving city. The roof had collapsed, leaving the interior a tangled mess of rubble and the scent of decay, but amidst the wreckage lay a treasure trove of

knowledge. Anya led the way, her nimble steps navigating the treacherous terrain, her senses attuned to the slightest shift in the air.

"There," she whispered, her voice barely audible above the rustle of the wind, pointing towards a pile of books, their pages yellowed with age. "It's a library. There might be something here."

They spent days sifting through the books, their fingers tracing the fragile pages, their minds racing with the

possibilities hidden within. They found fragments of

historical records, remnants of scientific journals, and whispers of a conspiracy that ran deeper than they had ever imagined.

The library, a repository of forgotten knowledge, became their sanctuary, their temporary haven from the unforgiving world outside. They hunched over dusty volumes, their faces illuminated by flickering candlelight, their minds grappling with the truth they were uncovering.

They learned about a secret government project, a shadowy organization that had been experimenting with a dangerous technology, a technology that had ultimately led to the apocalypse. They discovered hidden agendas, whispered conspiracies, and the chilling realization that the world they knew had been a carefully constructed illusion.

Each new piece of information was a step closer to the truth, but it also brought with it a heavy burden. The weight of knowledge, the burden of responsibility, pressed down on them, forcing them to confront the dark underbelly of human nature.

The library became a place of both discovery and despair, a testament to the power of human ingenuity and the depths of human corruption. As they delved deeper into the archives, they realized that the truth was more complex, more

terrifying, than they had ever imagined.

The search for truth was a dangerous game, a labyrinthine journey through a world where the lines between right and wrong were blurred, where hope was a fragile flame

threatened by the winds of despair. But Lila and her allies were determined to persevere, their resolve fueled by the knowledge that their survival, their very existence, depended on uncovering the truth.

They knew the risks, the dangers that lurked in the shadows, but they were willing to face them. For they had seen the darkness, the depths of human depravity, and they were determined to bring light to the world, to expose the truth, no matter the cost.

Their journey was far from over, but they had found their purpose, their reason for surviving. They were the guardians of truth, the keepers of the flame, and they would not rest until the world knew the truth, no matter how painful it

might be. The search for truth had begun, and it would shape their destinies, their very souls.

The Power of Unity

The weight of betrayal hung heavy in the air, a suffocating blanket of mistrust that threatened to smother any remaining hope. Lila, with a heart that ached with a mixture of anger and disbelief, watched as the group she had considered her family shattered into fragments. The revelation of Ethan's deceit, his carefully constructed facade of leadership

crumbling to reveal a self-serving manipulator, had ripped apart the fragile unity they had painstakingly built.

The whispers of dissent, once muted by a shared sense of purpose, now erupted into open accusations and bitter

recriminations. The survivors, each carrying their own scars and burdens, were now driven by fear and suspicion, their fragile trust in each other replaced by a cold cynicism.

Lila, her own past wounds festering in the wake of betrayal, recognized the familiar sting of disillusionment. She had seen this before, the descent into chaos and distrust that had consumed the world before the apocalypse. She had vowed never to fall into that darkness again, yet here she was, caught in the same vicious cycle.

But even in the face of such despair, a spark of defiance flickered within her. Lila knew that succumbing to cynicism would only perpetuate the cycle of destruction. She refused to let the darkness win. She needed to find a way to rebuild, not just for herself, but for all those who remained.

Her gaze fell upon the faces of the survivors who had stayed by her side, their expressions reflecting a mixture of hurt, anger, and a stubborn refusal to succumb to despair. In their shared pain, she saw a glimmer of hope, a testament to the

resilience of the human spirit. They had lost their faith in Ethan, but not in each other.

"We can't let him win," Lila declared, her voice ringing with a newfound strength. "He wants us to fight amongst ourselves, to tear each other apart. But we are stronger together. We have to find a way to heal these wounds, to rebuild our trust, and move forward."

Her words, charged with conviction, cut through the cloud of negativity. The survivors, each wrestling with their own demons, looked at each other, a silent acknowledgment passing between them. They had lost something precious, but they could not afford to lose everything.

They were survivors, bound by a shared experience of loss and a desperate need to forge a better future. They might have been shattered, but the pieces of their unity remained, ready to be pieced together. And Lila, determined to honor the memory of those who had fallen, knew that she had to be the one to lead them back from the brink.

A plan began to form in her mind, a strategy not only for survival, but for rebuilding trust and forging a new kind of community, one where the wounds of the past could heal and the seeds of hope could take root.

She knew that it wouldn't be easy. The scars of betrayal ran deep, and their journey would be fraught with danger. But they had to try. The world was a harsh and unforgiving place, and their only chance of survival lay in their ability to work together, to overcome their past grievances and

embrace the power of unity.

"We will find the truth," Lila affirmed, her gaze unwavering. "We will expose the conspiracy and bring those responsible to justice. But most importantly, we will learn from our

mistakes and build a better future, a future where trust is a cornerstone, and unity is our greatest strength."

Her words echoed in the silence, a faint whisper of hope that resonated deep within the hearts of those who had gathered around her. They might be broken, but they were not

defeated. They had a shared purpose, a common enemy, and a desperate need to survive. And that, Lila knew, was a powerful foundation upon which to rebuild.

The journey ahead would be fraught with challenges, but Lila was determined to lead them, to guide them toward a future where the shifting sands of trust could finally settle into a solid foundation of unity. The road ahead was long and uncertain, but for the first time in a long time, a flicker of hope, born from the ashes of betrayal, began to illuminate the path forward.

A Moment of Revelation

The air hung heavy with the scent of decay and despair as Lila crept through the abandoned city. The once-thriving metropolis had been reduced to a ghost town, its towering skyscrapers now skeletal giants, their windows vacant eyes staring out at a world consumed by dust and decay. Every step she took sent a cascade of debris crunching beneath her boots, a constant reminder of the world that had been and the world that now was. She clutched the worn, leather-bound journal tightly in her hand, its pages filled with cryptic

entries, fragments of a truth that had long been buried.

Lila had always been a survivor, a ghost flitting through the ruins, scavenging for whatever she could find to stay alive.

But lately, something had shifted within her, a hunger for something more than mere existence. The journal, a

discovery amidst the rubble of a long-forgotten library, had awakened a dormant sense of purpose within her. It spoke of a conspiracy, a chilling plot that had led to the apocalypse, a deliberate act of destruction rather than a tragic accident.

As she made her way through the labyrinthine streets, she thought back to the day she had found the journal. It had been tucked away in a hidden compartment within a

crumbling bookshelf, its pages yellowed and brittle with age.

She had deciphered the faded ink, piecing together the fragmented narrative, the whispers of a truth that had been silenced for far too long. It was a truth that had the power to shatter the fragile hope that still clung to the remnants of humanity.

Her heart pounded against her ribs as she reached the meeting point, a dilapidated warehouse on the outskirts of

the city. It was a haven for a group of survivors, led by a charismatic figure named Ethan, whose hope-filled words had drawn her in like a moth to a flickering flame. She had found a semblance of normalcy within their ranks, a sense of belonging she had craved for so long. But beneath the facade of unity, Lila sensed a simmering undercurrent of suspicion, a constant reminder that trust was a fragile commodity in this new world.

Lila approached the warehouse cautiously, her senses

heightened, her hand instinctively reaching for the rusty blade tucked into her belt. She had learned to be wary, to anticipate the unexpected, to read the subtle signs of danger that lurked in every shadow. She stepped through the gaping doorway, her eyes scanning the dimly lit interior, searching for any hint of trouble. The group was gathered in the center of the room, their faces illuminated by the flickering light of a salvaged kerosene lamp.

A wave of relief washed over her, but the relief was fleeting, overshadowed by a growing unease. Ethan was standing in the center of the group, his face etched with a mixture of concern and determination. He was a natural leader, his presence commanding respect, his words carrying a weight of authority. But beneath the surface, Lila sensed something amiss, a subtle shift in his demeanor that she couldn't quite place.

"We have something important to share," Ethan announced, his voice echoing through the cavernous space. "Something that could change everything."

A collective gasp rippled through the group as Ethan reached into his backpack and pulled out a weathered, leather-bound volume. Lila's heart leaped into her throat, a cold dread spreading through her veins. It was the same journal she had found, the one that held the secrets of the apocalypse, the

one that threatened to unravel the fragile fabric of their world.

Ethan carefully opened the journal, revealing the faded ink that spoke of conspiracies and betrayals. As he read the chilling words aloud, a wave of silence descended upon the group, the only sound the crackling of the kerosene lamp and the murmur of wind whistling through the cracks in the walls. Lila's gaze darted around the room, taking in the

reactions of her fellow survivors. Some were wide-eyed with shock, their faces pale with fear. Others, like Ethan, seemed to bear the weight of the revelation with a stoic calm, their expressions unreadable.

"The truth," Ethan said, his voice laced with a newfound urgency, "is far more sinister than we ever imagined."

Lila felt a sudden wave of dizziness as the pieces of the puzzle began to fall into place. She had long suspected that Ethan held back information, that he was guarding a secret that threatened to unravel the fragile trust they had built together. Now, as she listened to Ethan's chilling revelation, she realized that her suspicions had been justified.

Ethan revealed that he had been a high-ranking official within the government before the apocalypse, a man privy to the dark secrets that had led to the destruction of their world. He had been part of the conspiracy, a willing participant in the plot to reshape the world in a chilling new order.

Lila felt a wave of nausea rise in her throat, the weight of Ethan's revelation crushing her like a tidal wave. She had trusted him, believed in his integrity, and now she found herself betrayed, her faith shattered into a thousand pieces.

"But why?" she asked, her voice barely a whisper, the words struggling to break through the suffocating silence. "Why would you do this? Why would you betray us?"

Ethan's gaze fell to the floor, his jaw clenched tight, his face contorted in a mixture of remorse and defiance. "It was a necessary evil," he said, his voice strained, barely above a whisper. "A sacrifice that had to be made to ensure the survival of humanity."

Lila scoffed, her anger rising with every breath. "Survival?" she spat, her voice dripping with venom. "This was not survival. This was control, manipulation. You were playing God, Ethan, shaping the world in your own image, and you were willing to sacrifice everything to achieve your goals."

The tension in the room crackled with unspoken accusations, the silence punctuated by the crackling of the kerosene lamp and the beating of Lila's heart. She felt a surge of anger and betrayal, but beneath the anger, a flicker of hope began to ignite. Ethan's confession had shattered the illusion of trust, but it had also revealed a deeper truth. The conspiracy was far more widespread than she had ever imagined, reaching into the very heart of the government.

"This is not the end," Lila said, her voice steady despite the storm raging within her. "This is just the beginning."

The survivors stared at Lila in stunned silence, their faces a mixture of shock, anger, and uncertainty. She had spoken with a newfound confidence, a resolve that surprised even herself. The journal, the key to unlocking the truth, had awakened a strength within her she had never known
existed.

"We're not going to let them win," she continued, her voice ringing with determination. "We're going to fight for the truth. We're going to expose the conspiracy and bring those responsible to justice."

Her words ignited a spark of hope within the group, a
glimmer of defiance against the darkness that threatened to consume them. They had been betrayed, their trust shattered, but they were not broken. They had a common enemy, a shared purpose, and a burning desire to find justice for the world they had lost.

As the first rays of dawn peeked through the cracks in the warehouse walls, casting long, eerie shadows across the dusty floor, Lila knew that their journey had just begun. The road ahead would be fraught with danger, riddled with challenges, but she was determined to face them, to uncover the truth, and to rebuild a world based on hope and justice.

The Weight of Choices

8

Chapter 6: The Shadows of the Past

The wind howled through the rusted skeleton of a building, a mournful
symphony echoing the emptiness within Ethan. He sat huddled against a
crumbling wall, his back stiff, his gaze fixed on the desolate landscape stretching before him. The sun dipped below the horizon, casting long, skeletal shadows that danced across the dust-choked ground.

He hadn't slept for days, the memories churning within him like a storm in a restless sea. The choices he'd made, the decisions he'd taken, they all came flooding back, each one a sharp, painful jab to his already raw soul. He had been a different man before the apocalypse, before the world had crumbled and the shadows of his past had become his constant companion.

He remembered the day the sirens wailed, a sound that now seemed like a haunting echo from a forgotten dream. Back then, he was a successful
businessman, a pillar of the community, respected and admired. But beneath the polished exterior, a darkness festered.

He was ambitious, driven by a hunger for power and control.

His greed had consumed him, leading him down a path of corruption and deceit. He had manipulated and exploited, his actions leaving a trail of broken lives and shattered dreams. The apocalypse had been a harsh wake-up call, a reckoning for his sins.

He'd watched as the world he'd known burned and crumbled. He'd seen the faces of those he'd wronged twisted in pain and despair. And he'd realized, with a sickening clarity, that the apocalypse had not only destroyed the world around him but also the world within.

The weight of his past choices pressed down on him, crushing him with an unbearable burden. He'd seen the fear in Lila's eyes, the flicker of distrust that he knew was justified. He'd seen the pain in the faces of the others, the wounds of his betrayal etched deep within their souls.

He'd tried to make amends, to offer his skills and knowledge to help them survive. But his efforts were met with suspicion, with a cold, hard reminder of his past. He'd become a pariah, a shadow of his former self, a man haunted by the ghosts of his own making.

Ethan closed his eyes, the wind whispering secrets in his ear. He saw the faces of those he'd hurt, their eyes reflecting the pain he'd inflicted. He heard their voices, their whispers of betrayal echoing in the silence of the ruins. He felt their anger, their resentment, a weight that pulled him down, deeper into the abyss of his guilt.

He couldn't undo what he'd done. He couldn't erase the past. But he could try to make things right. He could fight to redeem himself, to prove that he was not the monster he had become.

He could help Lila and the others, guide them towards the truth, and hopefully, earn their forgiveness.

The wind died down, leaving behind a chilling silence. Ethan opened his eyes, his gaze fixed on the horizon. The sun had set, leaving behind a sky painted in shades of crimson and amber. He stood up, his body stiff from sitting still for so long. He knew that the journey ahead was fraught with dangers, that the scars of the past wouldn't heal easily.

But he was determined to face them. He would walk into the shadows of his past, confront the ghosts that haunted him, and fight for a chance at redemption. He had to, not only for himself but for Lila and the others, for the hope of a future that was worth fighting for. He would embrace the weight of his choices, learn from his mistakes, and emerge from the ruins a changed man, a man who could finally face the dawn with hope and a heart open to forgiveness.

The Scars of Betrayal

The air hung heavy with unspoken words, a suffocating blanket of tension that permeated the makeshift camp. The campfire crackled, casting flickering shadows on the faces of the survivors, each one etched with a mixture of anger, fear, and a lingering sense of betrayal. Lila, her hands clenched tightly around a chipped mug, watched the flames dance, her mind replaying the events of the past few days. Ethan, the leader they had trusted with their lives, had revealed a dark secret, a betrayal that had shattered their fragile sense of unity.

The revelation had been a gut punch, leaving them reeling in disbelief. Ethan had been more than just a leader; he had been a beacon of hope in a world shrouded in darkness. He had promised them safety, a chance to rebuild their lives, a future where they could find solace from the horrors they had witnessed. Now, that future felt like a distant mirage, fading with each passing moment.

"He wasn't who we thought he was," whispered Maya, her voice laced with pain and disillusionment. She had been the closest to Ethan, a confidante, a partner in his mission. Her gaze, filled with sorrow and a flicker of rage, met Lila's, the unspoken question hanging in the air.

Lila understood the unspoken. Ethan's betrayal was a wound that cut deep, a festering sore that threatened to consume them. It was not just the betrayal itself, but the weight of the unspoken truth, the realization that even in this desperate world, trust was a rare and fragile commodity.

"He was protecting us," said Mark, his voice gruff, his words tinged with a misplaced loyalty. He had always been the pragmatic one, the voice of reason, the one who believed in the power of logic and practicality. He was grappling with the realization that sometimes, logic was not enough, and trust was the most precious currency of all.

Lila's gaze drifted towards the ruins of a once-thriving city, a stark reminder of the fragile nature of human existence. The apocalypse had not only ripped apart the fabric of society but had also fractured the very foundation of human trust. She had learned that the harsh realities of survival could warp even the most noble of souls, pushing them to the edge of their humanity.

"He was protecting his secrets," Lila countered, her voice quiet but resolute. "Secrets that could have put us all at risk."

The tension in the camp grew thick, a palpable force that threatened to suffocate them. Ethan's betrayal was a wound that had yet to heal, a festering sore that had infected their shared hope. They were grappling with the realization that even in this desolate world, the human heart remained susceptible to the darkness.

"What do we do now?" asked Sarah, her voice trembling, her eyes wide with fear.

There were no easy answers. The scars of betrayal ran deep, leaving them vulnerable, questioning their very instincts. The journey ahead seemed shrouded in uncertainty, a path littered with doubts and dangers.

They had gathered around the campfire, drawn together by a shared need for solace, for a sense of purpose in a world that seemed determined to tear them apart. Yet, the flames danced, oblivious to their pain, their despair. The fire, a symbol of hope, seemed to mock them, a reminder that even in the face of darkness, life could find a way to persist.

"We move forward," said Lila, her voice stronger than she felt. "We find the truth. We find justice. We find a way to heal."

Her words, though laced with uncertainty, offered a sliver of hope. The weight of Ethan's betrayal was heavy, but they could not allow it to crush them. They had to pick up the pieces, piece by piece, and rebuild their trust, their sense of purpose, their shared belief in the power of human resilience.

The silence that followed was heavy, filled with the unspoken weight of their pain. But within that silence, there was a flicker of resolve, a shared determination to keep moving forward, to face the darkness with unwavering resolve. They had lost their trust, but they had not lost their hope.

The next few days were a blur of activity, a desperate scramble to restore some semblance of order. They debated their options, their voices echoing in the desolate ruins of a once-thriving city. Some, like Mark, clung to the remnants of their trust, hoping that Ethan's betrayal was a temporary lapse in judgment. Others, like Maya, remained skeptical, unable to forgive the wounds inflicted upon their fragile sense of unity.

Lila found herself caught in the middle, torn between the loyalty she felt for Ethan and the growing suspicion that had taken root in her heart. She had known Ethan for a short time, but she had sensed something genuine in his eyes, a spark of humanity that had ignited a flicker of hope within her. But now, that spark seemed to have dimmed, replaced by a chilling shadow of doubt.

"He had a reason," she argued, trying to convince herself as

much as the others. "He had to protect us, even if it meant hiding the truth."

But even as she spoke, a voice within her whispered doubt, a nagging suspicion that Ethan's reasons were not as noble as she wished to believe.

The group spent days scouring the ruins, searching for any trace of Ethan's past, trying to understand his actions. They found fragments of information, scraps of a life lived before the apocalypse, glimpses of a man consumed by secrets and haunted by a past he could not escape. But those fragments, pieced together like a shattered mosaic, only added to the mystery surrounding Ethan's betrayal.

"Maybe he's right," said Mark, his voice tinged with a hint of desperation. "Maybe we are better off not knowing the truth."

Lila shook her head, her eyes fixed on the smoldering ruins.

She couldn't accept that answer. The truth was a burden, a responsibility they had to shoulder. To bury their heads in the sand was to deny the very essence of their humanity.

"We deserve to know," she declared, her voice firm, her resolve unwavering. "We have a right to the truth."

The group remained divided, their trust fractured, their sense of purpose tested. The road ahead seemed treacherous, a journey into the heart of darkness, a quest for answers that could very well tear them apart.

They continued their journey, the scars of betrayal etched on their hearts, their souls weary but their determination unyielding. They had to find the truth, not just for themselves, but for the future of their world. The weight of the apocalypse was heavy, but the weight of betrayal was a

burden they had to carry, a constant reminder that even in a world shrouded in darkness, the human heart remained a complex, unpredictable, and often treacherous terrain.

A Chance for Redemption

The air hung thick with the scent of decay and the weight of unspoken words. Ethan stood awkwardly, his hands clasped behind his back, as Lila and her group gathered around a flickering fire. The warmth of the flames offered a meager comfort against the chill of the night, but it couldn't erase the tension that crackled in the air, a stark contrast to the crackling fire.

Lila, her gaze fixed on the flames, knew that Ethan's presence was a test. He had betrayed their trust, his actions a scar that ran deep, threatening to fracture the fragile unity they had forged. But she saw in his eyes a flicker of remorse, a glimmer of the man she had once believed him to be.

"I understand if you don't trust me," Ethan finally spoke, his voice a low rumble. "I know what I did, and I'm not here to ask for your forgiveness. I'm here to help. You need

information, and I know where to find it. Let me help you find the truth."

His words were sincere, tinged with a desperation that touched Lila's heart. She knew he was not the only one who had been forced to make difficult choices in this desolate world. She had faced her own demons, the specter of her past haunting her every step. But the betrayal ran deep, a chasm that couldn't be easily bridged.

"I'm not sure I can trust you, Ethan," Lila admitted, her voice flat. "What guarantees that you won't turn on us again?"

He sighed, the sound heavy with regret. "I know I've earned your distrust, Lila. But I beg you, give me a chance to prove

myself. I want to make things right. I want to help you find the truth, expose those who are responsible for this

nightmare."

The others remained silent, their faces a mixture of

skepticism and uncertainty. Ethan, ever the pragmatist,

understood their hesitation. He had done them wrong, and earning their trust back would be a long and arduous journey.

"I can't force your forgiveness," Ethan said, his voice a whisper. "But I need you to understand, the truth needs to be revealed. We all need to know what happened, why our world ended. And I know, I know that we can find it

together."

Lila met his gaze, her heart a battlefield of emotions. The pain of his betrayal was still fresh, but she couldn't deny the truth that he was right. The world was shrouded in darkness, and the only way to find a path to redemption, to a better future, was to shed light on the shadows of the past.

"Alright, Ethan," she said, her voice firm but laced with a note of caution. "We'll give you a chance. But you will have to earn our trust back, every step of the way. We're not blind to your past, but we're willing to see if you've changed."

A flicker of hope ignited in Ethan's eyes. "I won't let you down," he promised. "I'll do everything I can to help. For you, for Lila, for all of us."

The fire crackled, throwing dancing shadows on the faces of the survivors. The future remained shrouded in uncertainty, but with a shared goal, a common enemy, they were willing to take another step towards the light. The journey ahead would be fraught with danger, betrayal, and doubt, but they were determined to unravel the truth, to confront the shadows of the past, and to find redemption in the ashes of

their world.

Ethan, though burdened by his past, had become an indispensable part of their quest. His knowledge of the pre-apocalyptic world, the secrets he held, became invaluable assets in their search for the truth. He had navigated the treacherous corridors of power, a world where manipulation and deceit were currency, and now, he was willing to use his knowledge to fight the very forces he had once served.

Lila, ever the pragmatist, realized that there was a reason for Ethan's change. It wasn't simply remorse, but a burning desire to make things right, to atone for his past. He knew that the apocalypse was not a natural disaster, but a carefully orchestrated scheme, and he wanted to expose those responsible, to bring them to justice.

The journey took them through a landscape ravaged by the

apocalypse, a testament to the destructive power of human ambition. They encountered remnants of the old world —rusted cars, skeletal buildings, and abandoned settlements, each a silent reminder of what had been lost. They faced danger from mutated creatures, remnants of a world that had mutated under the radioactive fallout, and from the
unforgiving elements, as if the very land itself was
conspiring against them.

But they found solace in their shared purpose, their unity a flickering beacon of hope in the midst of despair. They were a ragtag band, a testament to the resilience of the human spirit, each carrying their own scars, their own burdens, but united by a common desire to uncover the truth and find redemption in the ruins of their world.

Ethan, despite his past, proved to be a valuable ally. His knowledge of the government's secrets, the hidden facilities, and the shadowy figures who had orchestrated the

apocalypse, became vital to their pursuit. He provided them with maps, coded messages, and insights that led them closer to the heart of the conspiracy.

He risked his life for their cause, putting himself in harm's way to gather information, to uncover the truth. He pushed himself to the limits of his endurance, driven by a desire to make amends for his past, to prove his worth, to earn their forgiveness.

Lila, watching him, saw the struggle in his eyes, the inner turmoil he was battling. She knew he carried a heavy burden, a guilt that clung to him like a second skin. But she saw also a flicker of hope, a glimmer of the man he had once been, a man who had sought justice, who had yearned for a better world.

They faced dangers, encountered enemies, and navigated

betrayals along the way. Each challenge tested their bonds, pushing them to the brink of despair. But they persevered, fueled by their shared desire for truth and their growing trust in Ethan.

They learned to trust each other again, to see beyond the shadows of their past and to recognize the potential for

redemption in the face of adversity. Their journey became a testament to the enduring power of hope, the resilience of the human spirit, and the potential for healing even in the

darkest of times.

The search for the truth, for a chance at redemption, was a journey that not only unearthed the secrets of the apocalypse but also revealed the depths of their own humanity. They found solace in their shared struggle, their connection forged in the crucible of adversity, a testament to the enduring power of hope and the possibility of redemption in a world consumed by darkness.

The Power of Forgiveness

Lila stood on the precipice of a decision that could shape the rest of her life. Ethan, the man who had once offered her a semblance of hope and purpose in this shattered world, stood before her, his shoulders slumped, his eyes betraying a

flicker of remorse. He had betrayed her trust, his actions leaving a gaping wound in the fragile fabric of their group.

The weight of his deception pressed down on her, a heavy burden that threatened to consume her.

The memory of his confession, the whispered words that shattered the illusion of their camaraderie, echoed in her mind. Ethan had confessed to manipulating the group,

exploiting their vulnerabilities to gain power and control. His actions were driven by a desire to create his own order, to build a new world in his image, a world where he could be the unchallenged leader. He believed he was saving them, guiding them towards a future free from the chaos that had consumed the world.

Lila knew that Ethan's intentions, however misguided, stemmed from a desperate desire for control in a world that had been ripped from under their feet. She had seen his vulnerability, his own inner demons, the ghosts of his past that haunted him. He had been a man on the edge,

desperately clinging to power in the face of uncertainty. His actions, born out of fear and desperation, had brought about a darkness that had seeped into the very core of their group.

The betrayal was raw, its sting still fresh. Lila couldn't ignore the hurt, the anger that churned within her. She had been vulnerable, trusting him with her life, her hopes for a future she had almost given up on. He had played on her

vulnerability, skillfully weaving a web of lies and manipulation.

Yet, beneath the anger, a flicker of understanding began to glow. She saw the remorse in his eyes, the genuine regret that painted his features. He was not a monster, but a man broken by the world he had lost. And maybe, just maybe, there was still a spark of good within him, a flicker of hope that could be salvaged.

The choice before Lila was agonizing. She could let the bitterness of his betrayal consume her, allowing it to fester into a poisonous resentment that would poison her soul. She could harden her heart, refuse to forgive him, and perpetuate the cycle of pain and distrust that had already ravaged their world. Or, she could choose to forgive him, to see the

humanity beneath the darkness, and offer him a chance at

redemption.

Forgiveness was not a weakness, but a testament to strength. It was a refusal to let the pain of the past define her future. It was an act of liberation, a shedding of the burdens that weighed her down. But forgiveness was not a lighthearted gesture. It was a difficult, arduous journey, a choice that demanded courage and a willingness to let go of the pain that had become so deeply embedded in her being.

Lila closed her eyes, taking a deep breath as she faced the weight of her decision. The images of her past, the memories of the horrors she had witnessed, the sacrifices she had made, flashed before her. She had lost so much, endured so much, and she was tired of carrying the weight of it all.

She looked at Ethan, his eyes pleading for a second chance, a chance to prove that he could be a different man. And in that moment, Lila saw a reflection of herself - a survivor, a survivor who had been broken and rebuilt, who had clung to hope in the face of unimaginable darkness.

She felt a glimmer of empathy for him, a recognition of his own pain and struggles. She understood that his choices had been born out of a desperate desire for control in a world that had fallen apart. But she also knew that forgiveness was not a guarantee of change. It was a risk, a leap of faith that could lead to healing or further heartache.

Lila knew that forgiving Ethan would not erase the pain, the betrayal, the consequences of his actions. It would not rewrite the past or change the course of their journey. But it could be a step towards healing, a step towards building a future where they could all move forward, together.

The choice was not easy, but it was a choice that she had to make. The weight of the world rested on her shoulders, and she had to find the strength to move forward, to forgive, and to hope for a future where the shadows of the past could finally be laid to rest.

A Shared Goal

The air hung heavy with the scent of charred earth and the faint tang of ozone, a constant reminder of the apocalypse that had ripped the world apart. We stood there, a ragtag group of survivors, united not by blood or shared history, but by a shared purpose—a burning need to uncover the truth. The truth about what had happened, the truth about who had orchestrated the destruction, and the truth about why we had been left to pick up the pieces.

Lila, the fiery soul who had ignited this spark within us, spoke, her voice raspy with exhaustion and resolve. "We've been through hell, each of us carrying our own scars, both physical and emotional. But we've also seen the worst of what humans can do, the depths of betrayal and the chilling realization that even in the face of extinction, some would seek to profit from the suffering of others."

Her gaze swept across the faces of our band, hardened by years of struggle and loss. Ethan, the former leader, his eyes betraying a mixture of shame and determination. Kai, the ever-optimistic mechanic, his face a canvas of determination and resilience. And then there was Maya, her sharp wit tempered by a quiet strength that had kept us going when despair threatened to consume us.

"But we won't let them win," Lila continued, her voice rising with a newfound strength, "We will not be defined by the darkness that swallowed our world. We will fight for a future where the truth is exposed and those responsible are brought to justice."

The whispers of a government conspiracy had haunted Lila

from the moment she stumbled upon that cryptic message hidden within the ruins. It had sparked a fire within her, a yearning for answers that had transformed her from a solitary scavenger to a leader, a beacon of hope in a world shrouded in despair.

Ethan, despite his past mistakes, had finally found his way back to us. His betrayal, a bitter pill to swallow, had left its mark. But his presence was vital, his knowledge of the government's inner workings a crucial piece of the puzzle.

"We've gathered the pieces," Ethan spoke, his voice laced with a sincerity that was hard to deny, "Bits and pieces of a larger picture that speaks of manipulation, deceit, and a chilling ambition for power."

He explained the whispers he'd heard, the hushed conversations amongst the elite before the world crumbled.

They spoke of a new world order, of a society where the weak would be culled and the strong would rule. It was a chilling vision, one that had fueled the fire within Lila, the need to fight against the shadows of the past that threatened to consume our future.

The journey ahead was perilous, fraught with dangers both tangible and intangible. We were facing an enemy shrouded in secrecy, an enemy that had mastered the art of manipulation and had played us all like puppets in a macabre game.

But we had each other, a bond forged in the crucible of survival, a bond that had grown stronger with each hardship we had endured. We had faced our demons, battled our inner fears, and emerged from the ashes with a shared purpose that transcended personal agendas.

"We may be a ragtag bunch," Kai interjected, his gruff voice filled with a surprising tenderness, "but we're not giving up. Not when there's still a chance to bring those responsible to justice, to ensure that what happened to us doesn't happen again."

Maya, her eyes filled with a quiet determination, nodded in agreement. "We're not just fighting for ourselves, we're fighting for the memory of those we lost, for the hope of a future where our children can breathe clean air and walk under a sky untouched by the scars of war."

The words hung in the air, heavy with meaning. It was a truth that resonated deeply within each of us, a reminder of the purpose that drove our actions. We were not just fighting for survival, we were fighting for a future, a world where the shadows of the past could not claim the light of tomorrow.

We knew the road ahead would be long and fraught with peril, but we had each other, and that was all that truly mattered. We had a shared goal, a common enemy, and a flickering hope that burned brighter with each passing day.

We would uncover the truth, no matter the cost, and bring those responsible for the apocalypse to justice. It was a promise we made to ourselves, to the memory of those we had lost, and to the future we so desperately longed to build.

The Trail of Clues

Chapter 7: The Heart of the Conspiracy

The air hung heavy with the scent of decay and desperation as Lila and her group traversed the desolate cityscape. The once-bustling metropolis now resembled a crumbling graveyard, its skeletal structures reaching towards a sky choked with ash and smog. Their journey had taken them through a labyrinth of shattered dreams, each fallen building a grim testament to the devastating power of the apocalypse.

They were following a trail of breadcrumbs - fragmented clues gleaned from scavenged journals, cryptic messages scrawled on graffiti-covered walls, and whispered tales passed down through generations of survivors. Each piece of information felt like a shard of a shattered mirror, reflecting a distorted image of the truth they desperately sought.

Their destination lay shrouded in mystery - a hidden facility rumored to hold the secrets of the apocalypse's origins. The facility was said to be a remnant of the old world, a place where the government had conducted clandestine experiments and forged the path to their dystopian future. Finding it was only half the battle. The facility was heavily guarded, rumored to be protected by advanced security systems and an army of brainwashed survivors.

Ethan, the group's charismatic leader, had mapped out the route based on a faded blueprint salvaged from an abandoned research lab. His eyes, usually ablaze with hope, now held a grim determination. He was driven by a personal vendetta, a burning desire to uncover the truth that had shattered his life before the apocalypse.

The air crackled with a palpable tension. The weight of their mission, the constant threat of danger, and the lingering doubts about Ethan's motives had taken a toll on the group. Lila, who had always been a beacon of resilience, felt her own resolve wavering. The journey had unearthed a darkness within her, a primal fear that gnawed at her sanity.

Their trek led them through a network of underground tunnels, a subterranean labyrinth hidden beneath the crumbling cityscape. The air was thick with the stench of decay and the suffocating silence, punctuated only by the echo of their footsteps and the occasional drip of water. Each shadow seemed to hold a sinister promise, a lurking danger that threatened to consume them.

They encountered a small group of survivors trapped within the tunnels, huddled around a flickering fire. Their faces, etched with despair and fear, spoke volumes about the hardships they had endured. They were the remnants of a community that had been decimated by a mutated creature, a grotesque beast spawned from the radioactive waste that permeated their world.

The survivors, in their desperation, had resorted to scavenging for food and water, resorting to acts of desperation to survive. Their eyes, once filled with the light of hope, now reflected a haunting emptiness. They were living proof that even in the darkest depths of despair, humanity could descend to unimaginable levels of savagery.

Lila and her group, guided by a sense of compassion and a deep understanding of the human condition, offered them a lifeline. They shared their meager rations, providing comfort and a flicker of hope in their desperate lives. They were a reminder that even in the face of utter devastation, the spirit of humanity could persevere.

The journey continued, each step fraught with danger. They navigated through a desolate wasteland, their senses on high alert, their every move measured and deliberate. The remnants of the old world - rusted vehicles, shattered glass, and dilapidated structures - served as a chilling reminder of the catastrophe that had befallen them. The air was filled with an unsettling silence, broken only by the howl of the wind and the unsettling chirping of mutated insects.

As they ventured deeper into the heart of the conspiracy, the trail of clues grew increasingly intricate. They had to decipher cryptic messages hidden in plain sight, piecing together fragments of information like a broken mosaic. Each revelation unearthed a new layer of the government's insidious plan, a web of deceit that stretched back decades.

They discovered a secret laboratory, abandoned but still intact, its equipment covered in a thick layer of dust and decay. The laboratory was once a bastion of scientific progress, now a haunted graveyard of ambitions gone awry. Inside, they found remnants of research projects, experiments that had gone horribly wrong, and documents that detailed a sinister plot to weaponize the very forces that had led to the apocalypse.

The weight of the discovery pressed down on them, heavy and

suffocating. They had stumbled upon a dark secret, a truth that threatened to shatter their fragile hope. The knowledge that the apocalypse had been orchestrated, not a random act of fate, left them reeling. The world they knew, the rules they had lived by, had been built on a foundation of lies.

Their journey had taken them to the heart of the conspiracy, and now they had to face its architect. The mastermind behind the apocalypse, a man known only as "The Architect," was rumored to be the puppet master behind a grand scheme to reshape the world in his own image. They had to confront him, to expose his sinister plan and hold him accountable for the devastation he had wrought. But the path ahead was fraught with danger.

The Architect was said to have an army of loyal followers, a legion of

brainwashed survivors who would defend him to the death. He had created a society built on fear and control, where the weak were discarded and the strong were rewarded with power and privilege.

Lila and her group were about to face a challenge unlike any they had

encountered before. They were not just fighting for their own survival, but for the future of humanity. They were standing on the precipice of a new dawn, a dawn that could either bring hope or despair. The choice, they knew, rested on their shoulders.

The Enemys Lair

The facility loomed before them, a monolithic structure of concrete and steel, its windows dark and lifeless. It was a stark contrast to the desolate landscape they had traversed, a reminder of a civilization lost. The air hung heavy with the metallic tang of decay, a suffocating reminder of the world that had been. Lila, her hand resting on the hilt of her

salvaged blade, felt a tremor of fear run through her. She had seen the remnants of the world before the fall, the echoes of its prosperity, but this place felt different, colder, as if it held secrets buried deep within its heart.

They had followed a trail of cryptic clues, whispers on the wind, leading them to this hidden fortress, a place cloaked in mystery and shrouded in whispers of conspiracy. It was said to be a place where the powers that be conducted their

nefarious experiments, a place where the truth about the apocalypse was concealed. Now, they were at its doorstep, their fate hanging in the balance.

Ethan, his face etched with a mix of determination and trepidation, gave them a curt nod. They had come this far, their journey forged in blood, sweat, and tears. There was no turning back now.

"Let's move," he said, his voice low and clipped, his gaze sharp and alert.

Lila, her gaze unwavering, took the lead. She was a shadow, moving with an agility honed by years of scavenging in the ruins. The others followed, their movements silent, their steps measured, their every sense on high alert.

They approached the facility's imposing gate, its metal bars twisted and warped, the remnants of a forgotten past. The rusted hinges groaned as Lila expertly manipulated the lock, her fingers nimble and practiced. It had taken weeks of preparation, weeks spent deciphering cryptic messages and navigating treacherous terrain, to arrive at this moment.

"We need to be careful," Ethan whispered, his voice barely

audible over the rustle of wind. "They are expecting us."

The air around them crackled with tension. The security system, dormant for years, had been reactivated, its sensors humming with life. The facility was far from abandoned, a stark reminder that they weren't the only ones searching for the truth.

Lila, her hand gripping the blade, scanned their surroundings. The air was thick with the scent of ozone, a familiar smell from the days of the fall. She could feel the weight of eyes upon them, unseen eyes lurking in the shadows, assessing their every move.

"They're watching us," she muttered, her voice a rasp in the eerie stillness.

The metal gate groaned open, creaking like a dying beast. They stepped inside, the sound of their footsteps echoing in the cavernous silence. They were surrounded by decaying walls, their surfaces scarred and pitted. The once-bright lights were flickering with the fading energy of a forgotten system, casting long and eerie shadows.

A cold, metallic silence descended upon them, broken only by the faint hum of machinery and the occasional creak of the decaying structure. The place was a chilling reminder of the past, a testament to a world lost and a future uncertain. They moved cautiously, their senses on high alert, navigating

the labyrinthine corridors. The air was thick with the smell of disinfectant and decaying flesh, a potent mix that sent shivers down their spines.

They came across a room, its walls adorned with faded propaganda posters and screens displaying distorted images of a world that no longer existed. The posters depicted a utopia, a world of peace and prosperity, a stark contrast to the reality outside.

The images were a chilling reminder of the manipulation, the brainwashing, that had been used to control the masses.

They moved on, venturing deeper into the bowels of the facility. The corridors grew narrower and darker, the air heavy with the smell of dust and decay. They passed through a series of rooms, each one more disturbing than the last.

They saw rooms filled with medical equipment, their surfaces stained with blood and grime. They found laboratories filled with strange and disturbing machines, their purpose unknown but clearly sinister.

They had stumbled upon a hidden world, a world where science had become a weapon, where the boundaries of morality had been blurred, and where human life had been reduced to nothing more than an experiment.

The air grew colder, the silence heavier. They were being watched, their every move tracked by unseen eyes. The facility pulsed with life, but not the kind they were accustomed to. It was a life fueled by fear, by manipulation, by the insatiable hunger for control.

They reached a massive door, its surface cold and smooth, its metallic sheen gleaming faintly in the dim light. It was a door that whispered of secrets, of power, of a darkness that lurked within.

Ethan, his eyes narrowed in concentration, reached out and pressed a series of buttons on the door's surface. The sound of clicking metal resonated through the silence. The door, its hinges groaning in protest, slowly creaked open, revealing a vast chamber beyond.

The room was filled with flickering screens, their surfaces glowing with an eerie green light. The air was thick with the scent of ozone and static, the smell of power and danger.

In the center of the room, standing in the shadows, was a figure shrouded in darkness, a figure that sent shivers down their spines. This was the mastermind, the puppeteer, the architect of the apocalypse.

The figure turned, revealing its face for the first time. It was a face they had never seen before, a face etched with a

chilling mixture of intelligence and madness. It was a face that spoke of power, of control, of a will to reshape the world in its own twisted image.

"Welcome," the figure said, its voice a low, hypnotic whisper, echoing through the cavernous room. "I have been expecting you."

Lila, her hand gripping the hilt of her blade, stared at the figure, her heart pounding in her chest. This was the moment, the culmination of their journey, the face of the enemy they had been chasing for so long.

She was prepared for a fight, for death even, but she wasn't prepared for the cold dread that gripped her as the figure revealed its intentions, a plan that went beyond destruction, a plan that aimed to reshape the world in its own twisted image.

The weight of the truth pressed down on her, a suffocating

weight that threatened to crush her hope. The world they thought they knew, the world they believed they were

fighting for, was a mere illusion, a carefully orchestrated facade designed to control them, to manipulate them, to keep them in the dark.

The enemy they had faced was not just a force of destruction, but a force of manipulation, a force that had been pulling the strings of their world for years, a force that had brought the world to its knees. The revelation was a chilling blow, one that threatened to extinguish the last flicker of hope within her.

But even as the darkness threatened to consume her, she knew she couldn't surrender. She had come too far, endured too much, to let the truth be buried again.

This was not the end, but a new beginning, a chance to fight back, to expose the truth, to reclaim their world, to rebuild it from the ashes.

The battle had only just begun.

The Face of Evil

The air in the facility was thick with a sterile scent, a stark contrast to the earthy aroma of the outside world. The fluorescent lights hummed, casting an unnaturally bright glow on the sterile walls. Lila, her heart pounding in her chest, felt a shiver run down her spine. This wasn't the crumbling, forgotten remnants of the old world; this was something far more sinister, a deliberate construction meant to control, to manipulate, to reshape. They had stumbled onto the heart of the conspiracy, a place where shadows danced and the truth twisted like a venomous vine.

As they navigated the labyrinthine corridors, the silence was broken only by the rhythmic click of their boots on the polished floor. The echo of their footsteps seemed to amplify the tension, a constant reminder of the unknown dangers lurking around every corner. The air was thick with an unnatural silence, a void punctuated only by the faint whirring of unseen machinery. It felt as though the very walls themselves were watching them, their surfaces reflecting a sense of cold, calculated purpose.

They found themselves in a sprawling chamber, its center dominated by a massive holographic projection. It depicted a world unlike the one they knew, a world where technology was not a force of destruction but a tool for control, a world meticulously designed to cater to the whims of a single, powerful entity. This was not a random apocalypse, but a carefully orchestrated event, a masterstroke of manipulation aimed at reshaping the world in the image of its creator.

A voice boomed through the room, its synthesized tones devoid of any emotion. "Welcome, survivors. It is

fascinating to see how easily you succumb to fear, to the desperate hope for answers."

Lila felt a chill run down her spine. She recognized the voice from the cryptic messages she had deciphered, the voice that had haunted her dreams, the voice that whispered of a world shrouded in shadows. She turned to face the source of the voice, her gaze meeting the cold, calculating eyes of a figure standing bathed in the holographic light.

The man, his face etched with a chilling mixture of arrogance and despair, was the mastermind behind the apocalypse. He revealed his plan, a twisted vision of a world where humanity was not free but controlled, where individuals were mere cogs in a grand machine designed for his own warped ideals. He saw himself as a savior, a guiding hand shaping a new world order, free from the chaos and inequality of the past.

His words were a chilling symphony of manipulation and delusion, a testament to the darkness that could fester within the human heart. He spoke of a world where chaos would be replaced by order, where the weak would be culled, and the strong would rise to rule. He believed he was ushering in a new era of prosperity, but his vision was marred by a chilling disregard for human life, a willingness to sacrifice countless souls to achieve his warped vision of utopia.

Lila felt a surge of anger, a burning hatred for this man who had orchestrated the destruction of their world, who had taken away so much and left them to face the harsh realities of a broken world. But alongside her anger, a glimmer of hope flickered. His plan, however twisted, had exposed the truth, the horrifying truth that the apocalypse was not a random act of fate, but a calculated act of malice.

As the mastermind unveiled his sinister plan, Lila knew they

had to fight back, not just for themselves but for the future of a world that could be saved. They were not just survivors; they were the last line of defense against a terrifying new world order, a world where freedom was a relic of the past, and the only future was one defined by his iron fist.

The weight of this realization settled upon them, a burden shared by the group. This was not just about survival; it was about confronting the face of evil, the chilling embodiment of human ambition gone awry. Their journey to uncover the truth had led them to a precipice, a moment where their fight for survival had become a battle for the very soul of humanity.

The Weight of Revelation

The air hung heavy with the scent of ozone and the acrid tang of burning metal. The flickering light of the emergency generator cast long, distorted shadows on the cold, concrete walls of the facility. The group, their faces etched with a mixture of horror and disbelief, stood before a holographic projection that flickered with a haunting, otherworldly glow. It was a map, a vast tapestry of interconnected data streams, each one a chilling testament to the meticulously

orchestrated destruction they had witnessed.

"It's not just... a random event," Lila whispered, her voice barely audible above the hum of the generator. Her eyes darted across the map, her fingers tracing the lines that connected a web of seemingly unrelated incidents. "It's a...a plan. A massive conspiracy."

A chilling silence descended upon the group. The realization struck them like a physical blow, the weight of the truth pressing down on their shoulders. Their world, already shattered by the apocalypse, had been torn apart once again.

This wasn't just a catastrophe, it was a deliberate act of malice, a calculated scheme that had been executed with chilling precision.

Ethan, the leader, his face grim with determination, stepped forward. "It's worse than we imagined," he said, his voice tight with anger. "They knew what they were doing. They knew exactly what would happen, and they didn't care."

The holographic map revealed a series of coordinated

strikes, targeting strategic locations across the globe. They had thought these events were random, acts of desperation or

misguided malice. But the data spoke a different language, revealing a sinister pattern of calculated destruction. The targets were not merely cities or military bases, but specific points of infrastructure, communication hubs, and research facilities. The goal wasn't just to destroy, but to cripple and control, to plunge the world into chaos and dismantle any hope of a future.

"They're not done," a young woman named Sarah, her voice shaking, spoke up. "They're still... they're still in control."

They looked at her, her face pale and drawn, the fear in her eyes a reflection of the terror that gripped them all. The implications were staggering, a terrifying prospect that twisted their stomachs with dread. The world they knew, even the world they were desperately clinging to, had been a lie. The truth, revealed in its stark, terrifying reality,

threatened to crush any remaining hope.

The holographic map displayed a series of interconnected data points, each one representing a key player in the

conspiracy. Hidden networks of influential individuals, government officials, and shadowy corporations, all working in concert to orchestrate a global catastrophe. The names were familiar, their faces etched in history books and news headlines. They were the power brokers, the titans of

industry, the men who had held the reins of power. But now they stood revealed, not as benevolent leaders, but as

architects of a global catastrophe.

A young man named John, his face pale and his eyes bloodshot, stumbled back. "They... they're still out there,"he said, his voice a mere whisper. "They could do this again.

They could destroy everything we've rebuilt."

His words hung heavy in the air, a chilling reminder of the precarious nature of their existence. The world was a

tinderbox, and they were living on a knife's edge. They had survived the apocalypse, but the threat was far from over. The conspiracy wasn't just a historical event, it was a living entity, a dark force that lurked in the shadows, poised to strike again.

"We can't let them win," Lila said, her voice now firm with resolve. "We have to tell the world. We have to expose them."

But the weight of the decision was crushing. The truth they had unearthed was a dangerous weapon, a double-edged sword that could cut both ways. The world, already reeling from the apocalypse, was in a fragile state. Revealing the conspiracy could lead to widespread panic, chaos, and even further destruction.

"But if we stay silent," Ethan said, his voice low and gravelly, "what's the point of all this? We survived all this, only to let them get away with it?"

The question echoed through the facility, a stark reminder of the moral dilemma they faced. Their mission, to uncover the truth, had taken them to this point. But the truth they had found was a terrifying burden, a responsibility they were ill-prepared to bear.

The weight of revelation, the knowledge that the apocalypse was not an accident, but a calculated scheme, pressed down on them with crushing force. It was a weight they would have to carry, a burden they would have to shoulder. Their journey, once a quest for survival, had transformed into a desperate fight for justice, a battle against an unseen enemy with the power to rewrite the very fabric of reality.

The Choice

The air inside the facility was thick with the scent of ozone and decay. The fluorescent lights hummed with an eerie, constant drone, casting long, distorted shadows that danced along the sterile walls. Lila, her heart pounding against her ribs, gripped the worn leather strap of her backpack, her fingers tracing the familiar grooves of the metal buckle. The weight of the truth

pressed down on her, heavy and
oppressive.

They had followed a trail of clues, a tattered map leading them through the desolate labyrinth of the facility, a ghost of a past that now lay buried under layers of dust and silence. Each step brought them closer to the heart of the conspiracy, closer to the secrets that had been kept hidden for so long.

They had discovered a room filled with computer terminals, their screens flickering with a spectral glow. Rows upon rows of data streams, cryptic codes, and chilling images flashed before their eyes. The evidence was undeniable: the apocalypse wasn't a tragic accident, but a deliberate act of destruction.

The mastermind, a shadowy figure known only as "The Architect," had orchestrated the event with meticulous precision. Their motive was shrouded in mystery, but the scale of their operation and the ruthlessness of their execution spoke volumes about their ambition and their depravity.

The weight of this revelation hung heavy in the air. They had stumbled upon a truth so devastating, so incomprehensible, that it threatened to shatter the very foundation of their hope.

The world they knew, the world they had been fighting to rebuild, was built on a lie.

They had to choose.

Should they expose this truth to the world, risking retaliation from the Architect's remaining forces and plunging the survivors back into chaos? Or should they keep the
knowledge secret, protecting their own survival while condemning the world to remain ignorant of its true fate?

The decision was a heavy one, a burden that threatened to crush them. Each member of the group grappled with the implications, their faces etched with concern and uncertainty.

Ethan, his eyes shadowed with a hidden turmoil, spoke first. "We can't let this truth die with us. This man must be stopped, his plans must be exposed." His voice, usually filled with an unwavering confidence, now held a tremor of doubt.

Lila, her gaze fixed on the flickering computer screens, felt a surge of anger. "He took everything from us, stole our future, our hope. We owe it to everyone who has suffered, to everyone who has died, to expose his crimes."

The others, their faces a mirror of her own conflicted emotions, voiced their own opinions. Some, haunted by the spectre of their own past, leaned towards secrecy. Others, fueled by a righteous fury, clamored for justice.

The room was filled with a cacophony of voices, each expressing the weight of their own experience, their own fears, their own desires.

Amidst the chaos, Sarah, her voice quiet but resolute, spoke up. "We can't let this truth be buried. But we can't expose ourselves to danger either. We need a plan, a strategy, a way

to make sure this knowledge reaches the world without putting ourselves at risk."

Her words cut through the tension, a beacon of reason in the storm of emotions. It was a plan, a way forward, a chance to navigate the treacherous waters of their newfound truth.

They spent the next few hours discussing options, weighing the risks and rewards of each possibility. They debated tactics, analyzed their resources, and strategized their next move.

The weight of their decision pressed down on them, but they refused to succumb to despair. They were survivors, they were warriors, they were the last flicker of hope in a world consumed by darkness. They would find a way, they would find a solution, they would find a way to expose the truth and bring the Architect to justice.

As they finally reached a consensus, a plan taking shape, Lila felt a flicker of hope rekindle within her. The darkness, the despair, the fear, they were still present, but now there was a glimmer of light, a sense of purpose, a fire that burned brighter than ever before.

They had made their choice. The fight for truth, for justice, for a future free from the shackles of manipulation, had just begun.

The Fight for Survival

Chapter 8: The Last Stand

The air hung thick with the metallic tang of blood and burning flesh. The facility, once a bastion of technological prowess, had become a tomb, its sterile corridors now stained with the crimson tide of a desperate battle. Lila, her heart hammering a frantic rhythm against her ribs, scrambled through the labyrinthine corridors, the stench of fear clinging to the air like a shroud.

They had underestimated the enemy. Their intel, gleaned from whispers and stolen data, had painted a picture of a highly organized, yet contained, force. They were wrong. The enemy was a hydra, its tentacles reaching far beyond their wildest estimations. They were outmatched, outnumbered, and trapped. The corridors, once echoing with the sterile hum of machinery, were now filled with the deafening cacophony of gunfire and the guttural roars of mutated beings, their eyes glowing with a malevolent hunger.

The first wave had come as a shock. They had been cautiously optimistic, assuming that the facility would be abandoned, a ghost town in the desolate landscape. But the silence was broken with a brutal efficiency, a torrent of armed soldiers bursting through the reinforced doors, their faces twisted with a chilling fanaticism. They had been caught off guard, their initial advantage quickly dissolving into chaos.

Ethan, his face grim, led the defense, his voice a calm counterpoint to the pandemonium. He moved with a practiced efficiency, his years of military training giving him an edge. He directed the group, deploying them strategically, utilizing the facility's layout to their advantage. But the enemy was relentless, their numbers seemingly endless. They pressed their assault, a relentless tide of bullets and roars, pushing them back, forcing them to retreat deeper into the facility's maze-like depths.

The facility, once a sterile haven, was now a battlefield. The cold, metal walls were scarred with bullet holes, the air thick with the acrid smoke of explosions.

The sounds of desperate pleas and chilling screams intermingled with the deafening roar of gunfire. Lila fought back, her fear morphing into a primal rage.

She was a seasoned scavenger, her skills honed by years of surviving in this harsh new world. She wielded her scavenged rifle with deadly precision, her movements a blur of agility and defiance.

But even her skills were not enough. They were losing ground, the enemy slowly but surely closing in. Their numbers were dwindling, each fallen comrade adding

to the growing weight of despair. The enemy seemed to know their every move, their every weakness. They were hunted, trapped in a web of their own making.

Then came the betrayal. It was a twist of the knife, a betrayal so profound it tore at the very fabric of their hope. One of their own, a man who had sworn to protect them, turned against them. His eyes, once reflecting the light of shared struggle, now gleamed with a chilling emptiness. He revealed their location, the enemy closing in on them with renewed ferocity.

The betrayal was a blow, a devastating shockwave that shattered their already fragile sense of unity. The trust, built on shared hardship and the desperate hope for a better tomorrow, crumbled. It left a bitter taste in their mouths, a taste of ashes and despair.

The fight continued, a brutal dance between survival and death. Their numbers dwindled further, each fallen comrade leaving a gaping wound in their hearts. They were outmatched, but they fought with the ferocity of cornered animals, their desperation giving them a fleeting glimmer of strength.

The facility, once a symbol of human ingenuity, was now a monument to their struggle. The flickering lights cast long shadows, dancing on the walls like wraiths of a bygone era. The silence, broken only by the echoing thud of gunshots and the groans of the wounded, felt as heavy as a tomb.

The fight for survival was no longer about a grand purpose, or the hope of a better future. It was a primal instinct, a desperate clinging to life, each breath a precious victory. The darkness seemed to seep into every corner, swallowing hope and dreams, leaving only a raw, desperate will to live.

Lila, her body aching, her heart a pounding drum of fear, pushed herself forward. She had seen too much, lost too much. This was their last stand, their final act of defiance against a world that seemed hell-bent on destroying them.

They fought with a ferocity born of despair, their movements fueled by the primal instinct for survival. But the enemy, a tide of relentless violence, seemed unstoppable. Each fallen comrade added to the weight of despair, each bullet a reminder of their dwindling hope.

Lila, her gaze fixed on the enemy, her hands gripping her rifle with a deadly intensity, felt a surge of defiance. This was her world, her battlefield. She wouldn't go down without a fight. Not without a final stand.

The air crackled with the energy of their desperation, the metallic tang of blood mixing with the acrid smell of fear. The facility, once a testament to human ingenuity, was now a tomb, a silent testament to the brutality of their struggle. This was their last stand, their final act of defiance against a world that seemed to be closing in on them, threatening to swallow them whole.

They fought with the fury of cornered animals, their movements fueled by a desperation that burned with the intensity of a thousand suns. Lila, her heart hammering against her ribs, moved with a deadly grace, each shot a testament to her survival instinct. But the enemy was relentless, a tide of violence that seemed to rise with each passing moment.

Their numbers dwindled, each fallen comrade leaving a gaping wound in their hearts. The hope that had once flickered like a fragile flame was slowly being extinguished, leaving only a cold, bleak reality. But amidst the chaos, amidst the despair, a spark of defiance remained. A burning desire to survive, a refusal to surrender to the darkness.

The facility, once a beacon of progress, was now a battleground, its sterile corridors stained with the crimson tide of their struggle. The enemy, a force of darkness and cruelty, pressed its relentless assault. But Lila and her comrades, their backs against the wall, their hearts filled with a desperate hope, refused to yield.

They fought on, each bullet a defiance, each breath a testament to their

indomitable spirit. The fate of their world hung in the balance, the outcome of this last stand determining whether they would succumb to the darkness or rise above the ashes, their will to survive burning brighter than the dying embers of a world on the brink of oblivion.

The Sacrifice

The air hung thick with the stench of burning flesh and acrid smoke, a grim testament to the carnage that had unfolded within the facility. Lila, her heart hammering against her ribs, scrambled through the wreckage, the echoes of gunfire still ringing in her ears. She had lost count of the bodies strewn across the floor, each a stark reminder of the

relentless enemy they faced.

Ethan, his face grim with determination, pushed past her, his gaze scanning the debris-strewn corridors. "We need to get out of here," he said, his voice hoarse. "They're coming."

Lila nodded, her gaze fixed on the flickering lights that flickered ominously above. They had been so close to

reaching the heart of the conspiracy, so close to unraveling the truth behind the apocalypse. But now, trapped within this concrete tomb, their hopes seemed as fragile as the flickering lights above them.

A wave of despair threatened to engulf her. They had been hunted, cornered, and forced to fight for their lives. She had watched as her companions, her friends, had fallen one by one, their blood staining the concrete floor. Her brother, Liam, his laughter, his warmth, his unwavering spirit, all extinguished in a flash of gunfire.

But even in the face of such overwhelming despair, a spark of hope remained, a glimmer of defiance that refused to be extinguished. She had a duty to fulfill, a promise to keep. She would not let the sacrifices of those she had lost be in vain.

As they pushed their way through the rubble, their footsteps echoing in the silence, a chilling truth settled over them. The enemy was not just a faceless, monolithic force. It was a reflection of the darkest corners of human nature, a twisted ambition that had devoured compassion and empathy.

Suddenly, a piercing scream ripped through the air. Lila froze, her instincts screaming at her to run, to hide, to protect herself. But the sound was unmistakable – it was Sarah, her friend, her confidante.

They burst into the room where the sound originated, only to find Sarah cornered, her back against a wall, her face contorted in terror. Three figures stood before her, their eyes burning with a cold, calculating malice.

Ethan charged forward, his gun blazing. Lila followed, her own weapon a familiar extension of her arm. They fought with a ferocity born of desperation, each shot a desperate plea for survival.

But they were outnumbered, outgunned. One of the attackers, a hulking brute with a crazed glint in his eye, lunged at Sarah, his fist connecting with her jaw with a sickening crunch. Sarah fell to the floor, her breath rasping, her eyes wide with pain.

The brute raised his fist again, ready to deliver the final blow. Lila, her heart pounding, felt a surge of primal instinct.

She threw herself in front of Sarah, her body shielding her friend from the impending blow.

A deafening roar echoed through the room. A flash of pain erupted in her side as the fist slammed into her ribs. She gasped, her lungs screaming in protest. She felt a wave of dizziness engulf her, the world around her spinning.

But she had done what she had to do. She had protected Sarah. She had kept her promise.

With a final, wrenching effort, she lifted her gaze to Sarah, her eyes filled with a mixture of love and a hint of apology.

"Run," she whispered, her voice weak but resolute. "Run, Sarah, and never forget what you saw here. Never forget the sacrifice."

Sarah's eyes welled up with tears. "No, Lila, I can't..."

Lila squeezed her hand, her strength fading. "You have to. Go! You have to tell the world what they did. You have to be the voice of those who can't."

With a surge of determination, Sarah scrambled to her feet, her gaze fixed on Lila's wounded face. "I will. I promise."

She turned and fled, her footsteps echoing in the silence, a desperate cry for survival.

Lila watched as Sarah disappeared, her own body fading into the darkness. The pain in her side had intensified, her vision blurring. She had bought Sarah time, but at what cost?

She knew that the enemy would not stop until they had eliminated them all. But she had made her choice. She had sacrificed her life to ensure that the truth would be revealed.

The world around her dissolved into a kaleidoscope of colors and sounds, a fleeting glimpse of a life that would never be.

But even in her final moments, she held onto a flicker of hope, a belief that her sacrifice would not be in vain.

As the darkness enveloped her, she whispered, "I have no regrets."

The Power of Hope

The air hung heavy with the scent of smoke and ash, a constant reminder of the devastation that had consumed the world. Yet, amidst the ruins, a flicker of hope persisted. Lila, her heart still raw from the recent loss of their trusted ally, Marcus, found a strange strength in the shared grief that bound them together.

The weight of what they had discovered pressed heavily on their shoulders – the chilling truth of the conspiracy, the orchestrated destruction that had ripped their world apart.

This knowledge, so horrifying, was also a source of unexpected solace. It meant that they were not simply victims of fate, but survivors, witnesses to a greater injustice, bound by a common purpose.

They had fought tirelessly to reach this point, braving treacherous landscapes and facing unimaginable horrors. Their journey had been marked by betrayals, loss, and the constant threat of death. Yet, they had never given up hope, each one drawing strength from the knowledge that their collective will could bring down those responsible for this catastrophe.

The truth, however devastating, gave them a sense of purpose. It was a flame in the darkness, a guiding light that refused to be extinguished. As they gathered around a flickering fire, their faces illuminated by the dancing flames, they shared stories of the past, of their families, their dreams, their resilience in the face of unimaginable hardship.

Ethan, his eyes reflecting the fire's warmth, spoke of a future where the sun would once again shine on a world free from

the shadow of the conspiracy. His words, laced with a quiet determination, resonated deeply with Lila. His belief in a brighter tomorrow, a world where truth and justice could prevail, fueled her own waning spirit.

Their shared hope, like a fragile seed planted in the ashes, began to take root. They clung to it, nurturing it with every act of kindness, every whispered word of encouragement, every shared meal. This hope, born from the depths of despair, became their anchor, reminding them that even in the darkest of times, the human spirit could endure, could rise above the ashes.

Each member of the group carried a piece of the hope within them. Anya, with her unwavering faith, believed that a

higher power would guide them toward a better future. Kai, the young scavenger, clung to the memories of his family, the hope that they might one day be reunited. And Lila, her heart still bruised by the past, found solace in the knowledge that they were fighting for a cause greater than themselves, a cause that could bring justice to the world.

This shared hope was their greatest weapon, a shield against the crushing despair that threatened to engulf them. It was a reminder that they were not alone in this fight, that there were others who believed in a brighter future, a future where the truth could set them free.

As the embers of their fire slowly died down, casting long shadows across the ravaged landscape, they looked up at the star-studded sky, a stark contrast to the darkness that

surrounded them. In the vast expanse of the universe, they found a sense of perspective, a reminder that even in the face of extinction, hope could endure.

Their journey was far from over, but they knew that as long as they held onto this shared hope, they could face whatever

challenges lay ahead. The future might be uncertain, the path to justice long and treacherous, but they were united in their pursuit of the truth, determined to bring the light of justice to the world they once knew. Their hope, a beacon in the

darkness, fueled their determination to survive, to rebuild, and to create a world where the echoes of ash would fade into a memory, replaced by the promise of a new dawn.

The Final Confrontation

The air hung thick with the smell of ozone and burning metal, a grim reminder of the destruction that had brought them to this point. Lila and Ethan stood face-to-face with the mastermind, their gazes locked in a silent struggle of wills. Years of living in the shadow of the apocalypse had forged a steel in Lila's eyes, a steely determination that matched the man's cold, calculating stare. Ethan, his face etched with the weight of his past and the burden of his choices, held his ground, his hand resting on the hilt of his scavenged blade.

The mastermind, a man whose name had become a whisper of fear in the wastelands, sat atop a makeshift throne crafted from twisted metal and shattered glass. He was surrounded by a cadre of loyal followers, their faces hardened by years of hardship and warped by the insidious ideology that fueled his reign of terror. The room, once a sterile laboratory

designed to push the boundaries of scientific progress, was now a twisted parody of its former self, a testament to the man's twisted vision.

"You've come a long way, haven't you, Lila?" The

mastermind's voice, a smooth and chilling baritone, cut through the tension-filled silence. "From the shadows of the ruins to the precipice of truth. But you still haven't grasped the true nature of the world, the way it must be. I have shown you a new path, a path to order, to stability. A world free from the chaos and the weakness of humanity's past."

Lila scoffed, her voice a sharp counterpoint to the mastermind's chilling pronouncements. "Order? You call this order? You destroyed everything we knew, everything we loved, all in the name of your twisted vision! You call

yourselves survivors, but you are nothing more than parasites, feeding off the misery of others."

The mastermind's lips curled into a cruel smile, his eyes glinting with a cold, calculating light. "You speak of misery? You haven't seen true misery, haven't felt the weight of a world teetering on the edge of annihilation. I have seen the rot, the decay at the heart of humanity. I have seen the futility of hope, the inevitability of our own self-destruction. I have shown you the only way to truly survive, the only way to rebuild."

"You didn't show us anything," Ethan's voice was low and dangerous, his eyes burning with a fire that rivaled the flickering flames casting long, dancing shadows across the room. "You stole from us, you lied to us, you manipulated us. You used our fear, our desperation, as weapons to build your own power. You took everything from us, and you call this survival?"

A low growl rippled through the mastermind's followers, their hands instinctively reaching for the makeshift weapons they carried. The tension in the room became palpable, the air crackling with the electric anticipation of a storm about to break.

"And you think you can stop me?" The mastermind leaned back in his throne, his gaze shifting between Lila and Ethan, a flicker of amusement in his eyes. "You think you can change the course of history? You are nothing but a footnote in the grand scheme of things. I am the architect of a new world, and my vision will prevail."

"We may be a footnote," Lila countered, her voice unwavering, "but we'll write a bloody one." She took a step forward, her hand reaching for the weapon strapped to her leg. "We'll make sure the world knows what you have done,

and we'll ensure that your reign of terror ends here, tonight."

Ethan mirrored her movement, his hand tightening around his blade. "We may be a footnote," he echoed, his voice a low growl, "but we'll write the last one. We'll make sure your story ends with the fall of your empire."

The room was engulfed in a chaotic whirlwind of movement. Lila and Ethan, fueled by a righteous anger and a desperate need to right the wrongs of the world, launched themselves into the heart of the enemy's ranks. The mastermind's followers, taken aback by the ferocity of their attack, scrambled to defend themselves.

The sound of metal clashing against metal, the crackle of energy weapons, and the guttural cries of the combatants filled the air. Lila moved with a deadly grace, her skills honed in the harsh realities of the wasteland, her every strike precise and lethal. Ethan, fueled by years of pent-up rage and a burning desire for justice, fought with the fury of a cornered animal, his blade flashing through the air, leaving a trail of fallen enemies in his wake.

As the battle raged, the mastermind watched from his throne, a cruel smile playing on his lips. He had anticipated this attack, had planned for it, and his followers were prepared. But he hadn't anticipated the tenacity of Lila and Ethan, the unshakeable belief in their cause, and the strength they drew from the very foundations of their humanity.

The battle was a brutal ballet of desperation and fury, a dance of survival played out in the ruins of a broken world. The air was thick with sweat, smoke, and the metallic tang of blood. Each fallen comrade served as a reminder of the stakes, the sacrifices they had made to get to this point. With every swing of their weapons, Lila and Ethan felt the weight of the world on their shoulders, the burden of hope resting

on their weary backs.

Amidst the chaos, the mastermind saw a glimmer of fear in Ethan's eyes, a flicker of doubt that threatened to unravel his resolve. He knew this was his opportunity, the chance to break Ethan's spirit, to shatter the last vestiges of hope in his heart. He raised his voice, a mocking laughter echoing through the room, "You fight so hard, Ethan, but it's all in vain. You are clinging to a dying dream, a world that no longer exists. Let go, embrace the new order. Join me, and together we will rebuild this world."

Ethan's hand faltered, his gaze flickering between Lila and the mastermind, his body wracked by a silent internal struggle. He saw the fear in his friend's eyes, the weight of their losses, the reality of their impossible odds. The mastermind's words, laced with insidious logic and a twisted promise of power, began to gnaw at his resolve. He had fought so long, so hard, but was it all for nothing? Was the world truly doomed to descend into the chaos the mastermind had predicted?

But then, he saw a spark in Lila's eyes, a flicker of defiance that ignited the embers of hope in his own heart. He

remembered why he had fought so hard, why he had refused to succumb to the despair that threatened to consume them all. He remembered the promises he had made, the dreams he had held, the future he had refused to give up on. He remembered the sacrifices they had made, the comrades they had lost, and the world they were fighting to rebuild. He remembered the love and the trust they had shared, the

unshakable bonds that held them together in the face of unimaginable adversity.

The flicker of doubt in Ethan's eyes was replaced by a steely determination, a fierce refusal to yield. He met the

mastermind's gaze, a silent battle of wills playing out

between them. His blade, his spirit, both stood firm, his voice a defiant growl that resonated through the room, "Never."

The battle raged on, each strike a testament to their resolve, each wound a reminder of the price of freedom. Lila and Ethan fought with the ferocity of cornered animals, their combined strength a formidable force that pushed back against the tide of the enemy's attack. They knew they were fighting against an enemy that seemed invincible, a foe that had orchestrated the very collapse of the world they once knew. But they also knew that they were fighting for

something bigger than themselves, for a future where hope could bloom again, a future where humanity could rebuild from the ashes.

The battle reached a crescendo, the room echoing with the sounds of clashing metal, the roar of the combatants, and the desperate cries of the wounded. Lila, with a swift and precise strike, disarmed the mastermind's second-in-command, her weapon a blur of motion as she delivered a killing blow. Ethan, in a moment of pure instinct, slashed through the air, his blade finding its mark in the heart of a loyal follower, a swift and merciless end.

The tide of the battle began to turn. The mastermind's

followers, seeing their leaders fall, began to falter, their resolve cracking under the weight of their losses. The room was filled with the sounds of retreating footsteps, the echoes of defeat ringing in the air.

The mastermind, seeing his empire crumbling around him, rose from his throne, his gaze burning with a cold fury. He reached for a hidden weapon, a device that hummed with a dangerous power. "You think you have won?" he roared, his voice laced with a desperate fury. "You think you can escape the consequences? I will burn this world to the ground, and I

will take you all with me."

Lila and Ethan, seeing the deadly device in his hand, knew they had to act fast. The mastermind's last stand was not a desperate act of a cornered animal, but a calculated move, a final act of defiance that could bring about the end of

everything they had fought for. They lunged forward, their bodies a blur of motion, their weapons ready to strike.

The final confrontation was a dance of death, a desperate struggle for survival played out in the shadow of a broken world. Lila, with a desperate lunge, disarmed the

mastermind, her weapon clattering to the floor. Ethan, in a final, heart-wrenching act of defiance, dove in front of Lila, taking the full force of the mastermind's last attack.

The explosion ripped through the room, a blinding flash of light that consumed everything in its path. Lila, blinded by the explosion, shielded her eyes, her body trembling with a mixture of grief and rage. When her vision cleared, she saw Ethan, lying motionless on the floor, his body shattered by the force of the blast.

The mastermind, his body twisted and contorted, lay near Ethan, his last breath escaping in a gurgling whisper. His reign of terror was over, his twisted vision brought to an end. But the price of victory was heavy. They had won the battle, but at what cost?

Lila, her heart heavy with grief, knelt beside Ethan's body, her hand gently brushing against his lifeless cheek. She had lost so much, so many, but she refused to give in to despair.

She knew that Ethan, in his final act of self-sacrifice, had bought them time, time to rebuild, time to heal, time to create a future where the scars of the past could finally begin to fade.

As the dust settled and the smoke cleared, Lila looked out at the ruined world, a world that had been forged in the fires of destruction, but also in the embers of hope. She knew that the journey ahead would be long and arduous, but she would not falter. Ethan's sacrifice, the sacrifices of all those who had fallen, would not be in vain. She would carry the torch of their dreams, their hopes, their unwavering belief in a future where humanity could rise again.

The world was in ruins, but so was she. And within those ruins, a new dawn began to rise. The last stand was over, but the battle for survival had just begun. And Lila, with a heart heavy with grief, but a spirit forged in the fires of adversity, was ready to face it.

The Dawn of a New Reality

The metallic clang of the escape pod's door sealing shut echoed through the sterile corridors of the facility. Lila, her heart pounding against her ribs, took a shaky breath, the air thick with the metallic tang of fear and relief. Ethan stood beside her, his face grim but resolute, his hand finding hers in a silent promise.

The weight of their discovery pressed down on them – the truth about the apocalypse, the web of deceit, the horrifying machinations of the government. But amidst the dread, a flicker of hope ignited within them. They had escaped, they had survived. They carried the truth, a seed of resistance against the darkness that had consumed the world.

The escape pod hummed, a mechanical lullaby as they hurtled towards the unknown. Through the viewport, they saw the stark wasteland, a tapestry of twisted metal and ash-laden landscapes. It was a world scarred, a testament to human folly, yet it held the potential for rebirth.

The others emerged from the pod, their faces pale with exhaustion but their eyes blazing with determination. They were a ragtag group, united by shared hardship and the burning desire to see a new dawn.

There was Sam, his youthful face hardened by the harsh realities of survival, his hands calloused from years of scavenging. There was Maya, her eyes reflecting a deep wisdom, her voice a soothing balm amidst the chaos. And there was John, a towering figure, his silence speaking volumes of the pain he carried, the burdens of the past.

They were not just survivors; they were the remnants of humanity, the seeds of a new world. Their journey had been long, arduous, fraught with peril. They had faced betrayal, loss, and the gnawing fear of extinction. But they had

endured, their resilience a testament to the indomitable spirit of the human heart.

As the escape pod touched down on a barren patch of earth, a sense of exhilaration washed over them. They had escaped the clutches of the enemy, but the fight was far from over.

They were free, but the scars of the past remained, etched deep into their souls.

They gathered their meager supplies, their weapons a grim reminder of the dangers that lurked in the wasteland. The wind whispered through the skeletal remains of trees, a mournful symphony of loss. The sun, a pale orb in the

polluted sky, cast long shadows, stretching across the barren landscape, a stark reminder of the emptiness that surrounded them.

"Where do we go now?" Sam asked, his voice barely audible above the howling wind.

Lila looked out at the vast expanse before them, the

desolation mirroring the emptiness she felt within. The

answer, she knew, lay not in a destination but in the shared hope they carried. "We go forward," she replied, her voice firm with determination. "We find a new home. We rebuild."

The others nodded in agreement, their faces reflecting a mix of fear and anticipation. The path ahead was shrouded in uncertainty, but they were united by a common goal. They were not merely surviving; they were reclaiming their

humanity, their future.

The weight of the truth, the burden of responsibility, pressed down on their shoulders. They were not just survivors; they were the keepers of a lost world, the custodians of a new beginning.

Their journey had only just begun. The dawn of a new reality was breaking, a fragile hope illuminating the desolate landscape. It was their duty, their responsibility, to ensure that it would never be extinguished.

The journey would be long and arduous, filled with challenges and sacrifices. But they would face them together, united by the shared dream of a world reborn, a world where hope would bloom anew from the ashes of the past. The last stand was over, and the fight for survival had just begun.

The Scars of War

11

Chapter 9: The Aftermath

The world was a canvas of devastation, a grim testament to the apocalypse's brutal touch. The once vibrant cities, now skeletal remains, bore the scars of war: crumbling concrete, twisted steel, and the haunting silence that hung heavy in the air. The sun, a pale and distant orb, cast long shadows over the ruins, highlighting the omnipresent dust that choked the air, a constant reminder of the cataclysm that had shattered their world.

Lila, her heart heavy with the weight of the truth, stood on the edge of the crater that once housed a bustling metropolis. She gazed at the remnants of a world lost, the enormity of the destruction a stark reminder of the fragility of life. The echoes of explosions, the screams of the dying, and the searing heat of the nuclear firestorm still lingered in her memories, a torment that haunted her waking hours.

The revelation of the conspiracy, the chilling realization that the apocalypse was not a random act of nature but a carefully orchestrated event, had left an indelible mark on her soul. It had stripped away the veil of innocence, revealing the depths of human depravity and the lengths to which power-hungry individuals would go to achieve their twisted goals.

The world was now a tapestry of despair, where hope was a fragile thread clinging to the tattered edges of reality. But amidst the ruins, Lila saw glimmers of resilience, flickering sparks of defiance in the eyes of those who refused to succumb to despair. Survivors, battered and scarred, were picking up the pieces, rebuilding their lives from the ashes.

As Lila walked through the desolate streets, she saw makeshift shelters

constructed from debris, rudimentary gardens coaxing life from the barren soil, and faces etched with a mix of grief and determination. The spirit of humanity, though bruised and battered, still clung to life, a testament to the indomitable will to survive.

But the scars of war ran deeper than the visible wounds. The survivors bore the invisible scars of trauma, the psychological wounds inflicted by the apocalypse. Lila had seen it in their eyes, the haunted look of those who had lost everything, the fear etched deep within their souls.

The fear of the unknown loomed large, a constant companion in this shattered world. Mutated creatures, the remnants of a poisoned ecosystem, lurked in the shadows, a constant threat to their fragile existence. The fight for resources, for food and water, was a daily struggle, pitting survivor against survivor in a desperate scramble for survival.

The conspiracy had exposed the dark side of human nature, the insidious thirst for power that could drive individuals to unimaginable acts of cruelty. The world was now a minefield of distrust, where alliances were fragile and betrayals were commonplace. Lila had learned the hard way that even in the face of shared suffering, the instinct for self-preservation could trump the most heartfelt bonds.

Yet, despite the bleakness, a glimmer of hope flickered in Lila's heart. The conspiracy had not extinguished their spirit, it had only forged it into an unyielding force. They were survivors, a testament to the strength of the human spirit, determined to rebuild their world, piece by piece, brick by brick.

The scars of war were a constant reminder of the horrors they had endured, a physical and psychological weight they would carry forever. But they were also a badge of honor, a testament to their resilience. They had survived, and they would continue to fight, not just for their own survival, but for the future of humanity, for a world free from the shackles of the past.

The journey ahead was fraught with challenges, but Lila and her fellow survivors were resolute in their determination to build a new future, a future where the scars of war would serve as a constant reminder of the need for peace, for unity, and for a world where humanity could rise from the ashes and reclaim its rightful place in the grand tapestry of life. The dawn of a new era was approaching, and though the scars of war were etched deep, the hope for a brighter future, however faint, would guide them toward a new beginning.

The Quest for Justice

The weight of the world rested heavily on their shoulders. They were no longer just survivors, they were heroes, the ones who had exposed the truth, the ones who had dared to fight back against the shadows that had consumed their world. But victory, as they had learned, was a bittersweet thing. It brought relief, a feeling of purpose, but it also brought the harsh reality of the task ahead: the quest for justice.

They had unmasked the perpetrators, the architects of this global catastrophe, but the road to accountability was a treacherous one. The world they had known was gone, replaced by a wasteland where law and order had crumbled. The remnants of the old world's systems of justice were mere echoes, buried beneath layers of ash and despair.

Lila, now standing at the precipice of a new era, felt the pressure of the weight of expectations. The survivors they had liberated, the ones who had been living in fear, looked to them for guidance, for a path towards healing. But how could they bring justice to a world that had already crumbled? How could they punish the perpetrators when the very fabric of their society had been shattered?

Their journey had shown them the darkness that lay within the human heart, the depths of greed and manipulation that could drive individuals to unimaginable acts. They had witnessed the cruelty of those who had profited from the apocalypse, those who had used the chaos as a means to further their own ambitions.

The group huddled together, their faces etched with the scars of their journey, their eyes reflecting the weight of the world.

They were a motley crew, bound by a shared history of trauma and a desire for redemption. Ethan, their former leader, stood humbled, the shadows of his past haunting his every move. He yearned to make amends for his past mistakes, to find some way to contribute to a better future. He knew he had a lot to atone for, and his words, once filled with arrogance, now held a newfound sincerity.

"We can't let them get away with this," Ethan said, his voice raspy from the harsh desert winds. "We have to bring them to justice, not just for ourselves, but for everyone who has suffered because of their actions."

"But how?" Lila asked, her voice laced with a weariness that mirrored the desolate world around them. "How do we bring justice to a world that no longer exists? What system of justice can we even hope to build?"

The question hung in the air, heavy and unsettling. They were facing a reality that seemed to defy logic, a world where the lines between right and wrong had blurred. The old rules no longer applied.

"Maybe justice isn't about punishment," Maya, a survivor who had joined them along the way, offered. "Maybe it's about truth. Maybe it's about exposing the truth to the world, letting people know what happened, letting them know that they weren't alone in their suffering."

The suggestion sparked a flicker of hope within them.

Perhaps justice wasn't about retribution, but about

accountability, about exposing the truth so that others could learn from their mistakes. They could become a beacon of light, a symbol of hope, a testament to the resilience of the human spirit.

"We need to document everything," Liam, a young survivor who had shown incredible courage despite his youth, said. "We need to write down everything we know, everything we've seen. It's the only way to ensure that the truth doesn't die with us."

The group nodded in agreement. It was a daunting task, but it was a necessary one. They would become chroniclers of their world, their stories a testament to the horrors they had endured and the hope that had kept them going.

They began by compiling their findings. They shared their stories, their observations, their insights. Every piece of information, every clue, every whispered rumour, was meticulously documented. It was a slow and painstaking process, filled with moments of grief and despair as they relived the trauma of their journey. But the sense of purpose fueled their determination. They were not just survivors, they were witnesses, bearers of truth, and their words held the power to shape the future.

Their message, once confined to the walls of the hidden facility, would now reach the wider world. They would use their story to ignite a spark of change, to expose the truth, to bring awareness to the injustices that had been committed.

They would not only seek justice for themselves but for everyone who had suffered as a result of the conspiracy.

They would use their voices to amplify the cries of the fallen, to ensure that the truth would never be silenced.

They knew that the road ahead would be long and arduous, but they were not alone. They were a force of unity, driven by a shared desire for justice and a belief in the power of truth. They had faced the darkness and emerged stronger, their spirits fortified by the unwavering belief in a better future.

Their journey had shown them the depths of human cruelty but it had also revealed the strength of the human spirit. They had found hope in the most desperate of times, and that hope, that unwavering belief in a better world, would guide their every step. Their quest for justice had begun, and they would not rest until the truth was known.

The Seeds of Hope

The news of Lila's group's harrowing journey to the facility and their exposure of the conspiracy spread like wildfire through the scattered settlements. What had been whispered rumors and hushed suspicions became undeniable truth, a beacon of hope in the ashes of a broken world. The

survivors, long accustomed to the harsh realities of their existence, were shaken to their core. Their world, already shattered by the apocalypse, was fractured further by the revelation of a manipulative force orchestrating their

suffering.

Lila and her allies, the survivors of that perilous ordeal, found themselves thrust into a new role – that of heroes. They weren't just survivors, they were champions, their story a testament to the indomitable spirit of humanity. The burden of leadership fell upon their shoulders, the responsibility of guiding a fractured world towards healing and redemption.

They became symbols of hope, their tale a whispered testament to the potential for resilience even in the face of overwhelming odds. Their journey resonated with every survivor, a testament to their own fight for existence. Gatherings in makeshift settlements morphed into rallies, tales of the conspiracy becoming a shared narrative of outrage and defiance.

Lila's group, with Ethan's quiet guidance, became a force for unity. They traveled from one settlement to another, sharing their story, urging the survivors to stand together. They emphasized the need to rebuild not just their lives but their society, to ensure that the mistakes of the past never repeated themselves. Their message was simple: they had faced the

darkness and emerged victorious, and so could they.

They established a council, a gathering of survivors from diverse backgrounds, united by a shared desire for a better future.

Their initial meetings were marked by suspicion, whispers of the past, and the fear of betrayal. But Lila, with her unwavering spirit and Ethan's quiet wisdom, led the way. They instilled a sense of unity and purpose, encouraging the council members to focus on rebuilding, on creating a world where the seeds of hope could blossom into a new dawn.

They set about tackling the daunting challenges of rebuilding a shattered world. The council tackled critical issues like food production, water purification, and resource management. The survivors, inspired by Lila's group, worked together to cultivate abandoned farmland, set up makeshift hospitals, and establish a network of communication.

They faced opposition, both from those who feared the change and from remnants of the old regime. However, the will for a better future was stronger. The message of unity spread, fueled by stories of Lila's group's courage and Ethan's leadership. The seeds of hope, planted in the fertile ground of despair, began to sprout, their tender shoots reaching for the light of a new dawn.

Their journey was far from over. They knew that the road to recovery would be long and arduous, riddled with challenges. But they had found a common purpose, a shared belief in a better future. They had faced the darkness and emerged victorious, their resilience a testament to the enduring power of the human spirit.

The dawn of a new era had arrived. The sun, rising over a world scarred yet not broken, cast its warm glow upon a new generation of survivors. They stood united, their eyes fixed

on a horizon filled with the promise of a better future, a future built on the foundation of truth, resilience, and a shared hope for a world free from the shadows of

manipulation. This was the last dawn, the beginning of a new chapter, and they would write it together.

The Price of Truth

The weight of the truth pressed down on them like the thick, choking dust that clung to everything in the post-apocalyptic world. They had risked everything to uncover the hidden history, the grim reality that the apocalypse wasn't a random act of nature, but a calculated, cold-blooded scheme. They had faced down the enemy, the twisted minds who sought to control the future, and they had emerged victorious, but not unscathed.

Lila, her eyes shadowed by a weariness that went beyond physical exhaustion, looked out at the devastated cityscape.

The towering structures that once held the promise of a bright future now stood as stark reminders of humanity's folly. Her heart ached for the life she had lost, the innocent lives that had been brutally extinguished. The truth had been a bitter pill, one that left a lingering taste of sorrow and regret.

Ethan, his usually confident demeanor now subdued, sat beside her, his gaze fixed on the horizon. His past, a tangled web of choices made in the desperate days before the

apocalypse, haunted him. He had been a pawn in the grand game of power, a puppet dancing to the tune of the

manipulators. Now, he was burdened by the knowledge of his role in the events that had unfolded, the realization that he had contributed to the very destruction he was now trying to undo.

The scars of the apocalypse were not just physical. They were etched deep within their souls, a constant reminder of the horrors they had witnessed and the sacrifices they had made. Each member of the group carried their own burdens, their own ghosts that whispered in the silence of the night.

There was Maya, her spirit shattered by the loss of her

family, her once-bright smile now a flicker of a forgotten memory. The weight of her grief was a constant companion, a reminder of the fragile nature of life and the fleeting nature of happiness.

And then there was Kai, the youngest of their group, who had lost his innocence in the fires of the apocalypse. He had seen things that no child should ever witness, things that had hardened his heart and replaced his youthful naivety with a chilling awareness of the darkness that lurked within

humanity.

They had won the battle, but the war was far from over. The world they had emerged into was broken, scarred, and filled with uncertainty. The truth they had uncovered had brought them closer, forging an unbreakable bond, but it had also instilled within them a profound sense of responsibility.

They were the survivors, the remnants of a world that had been systematically destroyed. They were the witnesses, the ones who knew the truth. And now they had to decide what to do with that knowledge.

Lila, haunted by the memories of her brother's death, was determined to ensure that the horrors of the past would never be repeated. She had seen firsthand the devastating

consequences of unchecked power and the dangers of

trusting those who promised a brighter future. She knew that the truth had to be shared, that humanity had to learn from its mistakes.

But the cost of exposing the conspiracy was high. The

enemy was powerful, their reach far-reaching, their influence deeply entrenched. Revealing their secrets would undoubtedly trigger a wave of retaliation, potentially leading to further violence and instability.

They were caught in a vicious cycle: a desperate need to expose the truth, balanced against the very real dangers that such action might bring.

The price of truth was not just measured in the lives lost and the sacrifices made. It was also measured in the emotional toll it took on their spirits, the scars it left on their souls. They had seen too much, endured too much, and the weight of their knowledge was a heavy burden to bear.

They knew that there was no easy answer. The path ahead was shrouded in uncertainty, the future a murky landscape filled with shadows and unknown perils. But they also knew that they had a responsibility to the world, a responsibility to ensure that the lessons learned from the apocalypse would not be forgotten.

Their journey had been marked by loss, betrayal, and despair, but it had also been a testament to the strength of the human spirit, the enduring power of hope, and the profound capacity for love that even in the face of utter devastation could not be extinguished. They were survivors, not just of the apocalypse, but of the darkness that had threatened to consume them. They had found strength in their shared purpose, in their unwavering determination to bring justice to a world that had been wronged.

The sun rose above the desolate landscape, casting a long, thin sliver of light across the horizon. It was a fragile, tentative dawn, a glimmer of hope in a world consumed by despair. They stood there, a band of brothers and sisters, united by the shared experience of suffering and the unwavering belief that a better future was possible. They had paid the price of truth, and now they were ready to embrace the dawn of a new era, a world where they could finally begin to heal, rebuild, and move forward.

The Last Dawn

The air hung heavy with a silent expectation, the desolate landscape stretching out before them like a canvas painted in shades of grey and dust. The remnants of the old world, skeletal structures reaching towards a sky choked with ash, stood as grim reminders of what they had lost. But amidst the desolation, a fragile hope flickered. A hope born from the shared experience of survival, from the enduring spirit of humanity.

Lila stood on a hilltop, the wind whipping at her ragged clothes, the scent of burnt earth and decaying metal filling her nostrils. She looked towards the east, where a faint blush of color began to paint the horizon. It was a sunrise, a simple act of nature, yet in this desolate world, it held a profound significance.

A hushed murmur rippled through the gathering of survivors, their faces etched with a mixture of awe and trepidation.

They had journeyed far, endured hardships unimaginable, and witnessed the darkness that dwelled within the human heart. They had lost loved ones, friends, and a world that had been their home. Yet, they stood here, battered but not broken, their eyes fixed on the dawning light.

It was a sunrise that carried a symbolic weight, a beacon of hope in a world that seemed destined for darkness. The survivors had fought for this moment, had clung to the fragile threads of their humanity, and now, as the light broke through the gloom, they dared to dream of a new beginning. A world where they could rebuild, heal, and create a future that transcended the ashes of the past.

Ethan, the leader they had chosen despite his past betrayals, stood beside Lila. His eyes, usually filled with a steely

resolve, held a flicker of emotion that mirrored the quiet reverence of those around them. The apocalypse had stripped them bare, exposed their vulnerabilities, and forced them to confront the abyss that lay within. They had learned, through pain and sacrifice, that survival was not just about staying alive, but about maintaining the very essence of what it meant to be human.

As the sun rose higher, casting long shadows across the shattered landscape, Lila felt a strange sense of peace settle over her. The scars of the past, the weight of her losses, the memories of the horrors she had witnessed, all seemed to fade into the background, their edges softened by the golden light.

"This," Ethan said, his voice roughened by the dust and the weight of his own past, "is the last dawn."

His words hung in the air, a declaration of hope and a

promise of a future that was yet to be written. The survivors, their faces illuminated by the rising sun, nodded in silent agreement. They were the remnants, the survivors, the ones who had dared to face the abyss and emerge, scarred but undaunted, ready to write their own story.

The journey that had brought them to this point was fraught with danger, betrayal, and sacrifice. They had faced a world turned upside down, where every step held the potential for death and every encounter carried the risk of treachery. They had learned to navigate the treacherous terrain of a broken world, to trust and to be betrayed, to fight for their lives and for a future they could barely imagine.

And now, as they stood bathed in the golden glow of the rising sun, they knew that the journey was far from over. The world was still in ruins, the scars of the apocalypse still fresh and raw. But within the hearts of these survivors, a spark of hope had ignited, a determination to build a better world, a world free from the manipulations that had brought about their downfall.

Lila looked out at the faces around her, at the raw strength etched into their features, the resilience that shone in their eyes. She saw the reflection of her own struggle, her own fear and her own hope. They were the survivors, the ones who had seen the depths of human darkness and emerged with their humanity intact. They were the ones who would rebuild, who would create a world that honored the sacrifices they had made.

The last dawn was a symbolic moment, a promise of renewal, a chance to rewrite the story of their world. They would carry the scars of the past, but they would also carry the memories of their shared journey, the bonds they had forged in the face of unimaginable adversity. They were the last dawn, a testament to the enduring power of human spirit, a testament to the hope that even in the darkest of times, humanity could rise again.

As the sun climbed higher, casting its warmth on the desolate landscape, Lila felt a sense of purpose stir within her. The journey was not over. The fight for justice, for a world free from the shadows of the past, was only just beginning. But she had faith, a faith in the resilience of the human spirit, a faith in the survivors gathered around her, a faith in the last dawn.

The Long Road to Recovery

12

Chapter 10: The Road Ahead

The survivors, scarred and weary, stood on the precipice of a new era. The echoes of the apocalypse still lingered, a haunting reminder of the world they had lost. The air hummed with a strange blend of hope and trepidation. The truth they had uncovered, the devastating conspiracy that had plunged the world into chaos, had left them with a heavy burden. Yet, amidst the ruins, a glimmer of possibility had emerged.

They were no longer just survivors; they were the architects of a new dawn. But the path ahead was fraught with challenges. The world they knew had crumbled, leaving behind a barren landscape of shattered dreams and broken promises.

Food was scarce, resources were dwindling, and the remnants of civilization teetered on the brink of collapse.

The scars of the apocalypse ran deep, etched into the very fabric of human society. Distrust, suspicion, and desperation gnawed at the fragile bonds of community. The survivors, hardened by their ordeal, struggled to rebuild a sense of unity, a shared purpose that transcended the fear and uncertainty that consumed them.

Lila, her heart heavy with the weight of the truth, recognized the daunting task before them. The fight for survival was far from over. The world was a canvas of wreckage, a testament to the destructive power of greed and ambition. Yet, she refused to succumb to despair. The echoes of the conspiracy that had nearly extinguished their hope now fueled a burning desire for change, a yearning for a future where justice and compassion would prevail.

The journey ahead was long and arduous, a constant struggle against the

remnants of the old world and the darkness that lurked within. They faced the specter of social unrest, the whispers of anarchy that threatened to unravel the fragile threads of unity they had painstakingly woven. Survival, once a desperate instinct, now morphed into a collective responsibility, a shared commitment to forge a new future from the ashes of the past.

The scars of betrayal, the wounds inflicted by those they had once trusted, remained a stark reminder of the fragility of hope. Yet, they found solace in the shared determination to rebuild, to create a society where the darkness they had faced would never again threaten to consume them.

They had faced the apocalypse, the ultimate test of human resilience. They had unmasked the truth, exposed the dark underbelly of power and manipulation. Now, they stood on the threshold of a new world, a world where the promise of a better tomorrow was a fragile but precious flame that flickered in the hearts of those who dared to hope.

The road ahead was uncertain, paved with the remnants of the past and the shadows of doubt. But they had the strength of their shared experience, the resilience forged in the crucible of the apocalypse. They had the memory of those who had perished, the weight of their sacrifice, and the unwavering belief that a new dawn could rise from the ashes.

They were the survivors, the torchbearers of hope, and the architects of a new world. They would rebuild, not with the flawed blueprint of the old world, but with a vision that prioritized compassion, justice, and the indomitable spirit of humanity. The echoes of the apocalypse would forever reverberate, a reminder of the darkness they had overcome, but they would also serve as a testament to the enduring power of hope.

The Future Uncertain

The journey ahead was a daunting prospect. The world they knew was gone, replaced by a harsh, unforgiving landscape.

They were adrift on a sea of uncertainty, the echoes of the old world fading into the dust-choked air. Yet, amidst the ruins, a flicker of hope persisted. The survivors, battered but unbroken, clung to the belief that they could rebuild, forge a new society from the ashes of the old.

They had witnessed the depths of human depravity, the desperation that could drive individuals to betray their own kind. Yet, they had also seen acts of extraordinary kindness, the resilience that sprang forth in the face of unimaginable loss. This dichotomy, this unsettling blend of darkness and light, defined their existence. They had learned to trust cautiously, to cherish the bonds of friendship, and to hold onto hope, however fragile it might seem.

The truth, however, was a double-edged sword. It had awakened them to the sinister forces that had orchestrated the apocalypse, but it had also revealed the fragility of their world and the precariousness of their existence. The weight of knowledge, of responsibility, pressed heavily on their shoulders. The fight for survival, they realized, was not just against the harsh realities of their environment, but also against the dark forces that sought to control and manipulate them.

Their journey, however, was far from over. They had a mission, a purpose born from the ashes of their past. They were not just survivors, they were beacons of hope,

determined to build a future where humanity could rise above the horrors of the past. Their goal was not just to

rebuild the world, but to reshape it, to create a new society based on compassion, equality, and a shared commitment to peace.

This wouldn't be an easy task. They faced a daunting array of challenges – resource scarcity, social unrest, and the ever-present threat of the remnants of the old world. The road ahead was paved with uncertainty, but the survivors, forged in the fires of the apocalypse, were determined to forge a new path. They would rely on their collective strength, their unwavering belief in the human spirit, and their shared dream of a brighter future.

Lila, once a solitary scavenger haunted by the ghosts of her past, had transformed into a leader, her voice a beacon of hope in the darkness. She carried the weight of the truth, the knowledge of the conspiracy, and the burden of ensuring that their journey was not in vain. She had become a symbol of resilience, a testament to the enduring spirit of humanity.

The journey to create a new world would be long and

arduous. There would be setbacks, betrayals, and moments of despair. But the survivors, now bound together by shared purpose, refused to succumb to the darkness. They would not allow the ghosts of the past to dictate their future. They would face the challenges ahead with courage and determination, knowing that the dawn of a new era was within their grasp.

The final scene, a symbolic sunrise casting a warm glow across the ruins, held a poignant beauty. It was a reminder that even in the darkest of times, hope could bloom, that humanity could find the strength to rise from the ashes. The story was not yet complete, but it held the promise of a new beginning, a world where the scars of the past would

eventually fade, and a new chapter in the story of humanity could be written.

The Legacy of Truth

The weight of the truth, a heavy mantle, settled upon Lila's shoulders. The world, though scarred and broken, was

slowly starting to heal. It was a fragile peace, a fragile hope, and she knew it could be shattered in an instant. The

whispers of conspiracy, the insidious web of deceit that had led to the apocalypse, were now a chilling reality. She

carried within her the burden of knowing, a responsibility to ensure that the lessons learned from the dark past would not be forgotten.

The new world was a tapestry woven from the threads of loss and resilience, a fragile unity built upon shared suffering and the collective yearning for a better future. The survivors had banded together, driven by a shared hope, a desperate need to rebuild, to create a world where the atrocities of the past would never be repeated. But the scars ran deep, and the specter of the past loomed large.

Lila, now a prominent figure in this nascent society, found herself at the heart of this delicate balance. She had emerged from the ashes as a beacon of hope, a voice for the voiceless, and a symbol of resistance against the darkness that had nearly consumed them. But the burden of leadership was a heavy one, a constant reminder of the responsibility she carried.

Her journey had been fraught with peril, her soul tested by the darkness that lurked within the ruins of civilization. She had faced betrayals, loss, and the chilling realization that even in the most desperate of times, human nature could be as treacherous as the wasteland itself. But through it all, she had clung to the flickering flame of hope, a relentless pursuit

of truth that had guided her through the darkest corners of the post-apocalyptic world.

Now, standing at the precipice of a new dawn, she understood that the fight was far from over. The seeds of greed, of manipulation, still lurked within the hearts of men. The world was a fragile ecosystem, one where the shadows of the past could easily creep back into the light, threatening to smother the fragile hope that had sprouted from the ruins.

It was her task, her solemn vow, to ensure that the truth of the apocalypse would never be forgotten. The world needed to remember the horrors, the manipulations, the devastation wrought by those who sought power and control at the cost of humanity. It was a warning, a testament to the fragility of civilization and the devastating consequences of unchecked ambition.

Lila, the survivor, the leader, the keeper of truth, knew she couldn't erase the past. But she could shape the future, ensuring that the lessons learned from the ashes would guide them toward a brighter, more just, and more equitable world. It wouldn't be easy. The road ahead would be long, arduous, and fraught with uncertainty. But with each step, with every

new sunrise, she would carry the torch of truth, illuminating the path toward a future where hope would not be
extinguished, but nurtured and protected for generations to come.

The Unfolding Story

The sun dipped below the jagged horizon, painting the sky in hues of bruised purple and burnt orange. The remnants of a dying world cast long, skeletal shadows across the
wasteland, stretching towards the dilapidated buildings that served as silent sentinels of a lost civilization. Lila stood at the precipice of a new dawn, her weary eyes fixed on the horizon. The weight of the journey, the burden of the truth, pressed heavily upon her. The revelation of the conspiracy, the orchestration of the apocalypse, had shattered the fragile remnants of her hope, leaving her with a bitter taste of
betrayal.

But amidst the ruins, a flicker of resilience remained. The group, battered but unbroken, stood together. They were no longer simply survivors, but a force, a testament to the
enduring spirit of humanity. They had faced the darkness, the shadows of doubt and the insidious whispers of betrayal. They had emerged from the ashes, carrying the weight of the truth, a responsibility to ensure that the horrors of the past would never be forgotten.

The road ahead stretched before them, a treacherous
landscape of uncertainty. The world was a shattered mirror, reflecting fragments of a lost past. The echoes of destruction lingered, a constant reminder of the fragility of civilization. They had faced monstrous creatures, mutated by the fallout of the apocalypse, and navigated through treacherous

wastelands where the very air seemed to whisper of decay. They had confronted rival factions, their desperation fueled by a struggle for dwindling resources, their humanity warped by the harsh realities of their existence. They had witnessed the depths of human depravity, the darkness that could

consume even the most hardened soul.

Yet, through it all, they had clung to a thread of hope. They had forged bonds of kinship, sharing their burdens and their triumphs, their vulnerabilities and their strength. They had learned to trust, to rely on each other, even when the world seemed to conspire against them. In the face of unimaginable loss, they had found solace in each other, a beacon of humanity in the darkness.

As they stood on the precipice of a new beginning, they were no longer just survivors. They were pioneers, the architects of a new world, a world born from the ashes of the past.

Their journey had been fraught with danger, their resolve tested at every turn, but they had endured. They had faced the darkness and emerged stronger, their spirits tempered by fire.

But the road ahead was long and arduous. The scars of the past would forever remain, etched deep within their souls. The memory of lost lives, of shattered dreams, would serve as a constant reminder of the fragile nature of existence. The struggle for survival would continue, the fight for a better future, a future where the mistakes of the past would not be repeated.

The echoes of the apocalypse lingered, a haunting reminder of the fragility of civilization. The scars of the past ran deep, whispering of the dangers of greed, manipulation, and the darkness that lay dormant within the human heart. They were not yet free from the shadows, but they carried within them the embers of hope. They were the architects of a new dawn, a world where the lessons of the past could serve as a guiding light. They were the last hope, the promise of a new beginning, a testament to the resilience of the human spirit.

Their journey was not yet over. The challenges that lay

ahead would test their limits, pushing them to the brink of despair. But they had faced the darkness before, and they had emerged victorious. They had learned that even in the darkest of times, the flicker of hope can be enough to guide them. They had learned that humanity's capacity for resilience is far greater than anyone could imagine.

The road ahead was long and treacherous, but they were not alone. They carried within them the strength of their convictions, the fire of their determination, and the unwavering belief that a better world was possible. As they gazed towards the horizon, a new day dawning on the scarred landscape, they knew that the story of survival, hope, and resilience had only just begun.

A New Dawn

The silence of the abandoned city was broken only by the gentle rustle of leaves as the wind danced through the skeletal remains of skyscrapers. Lila stood on the precipice of a rooftop, gazing out at the sprawling wasteland that had once been a thriving metropolis. The setting sun cast long, melancholic shadows across the broken asphalt, painting the scene in hues of orange and crimson.

She had always been drawn to the beauty of sunsets, even in this bleak world. It was a reminder that even in the darkest of times, there was still a glimmer of hope, a promise of a new beginning. Today, that hope felt stronger than ever before.

The journey to uncover the truth had been arduous, fraught with danger and betrayal. They had lost friends along the way, their sacrifices etched into Lila's memory as a testament to the resilience of the human spirit. And yet, they had

persevered, their shared determination burning like a beacon in the desolate landscape.

Now, as they stood on the edge of a new era, a sense of accomplishment washed over Lila. The conspiracy had been exposed, the perpetrators apprehended, and the weight of their burden lifted. They had fought against the darkness, not just for their own survival, but for the future of humanity.

They were no longer just survivors, clinging to the remnants of a shattered world. They were the pioneers of a new dawn, the architects of a society built on the ashes of the old. And as the last rays of sunlight faded into the horizon, a sense of quiet hope settled over Lila.

The road ahead would be long and treacherous. The scars of the apocalypse ran deep, and the challenges of rebuilding a shattered world were immense. They would face resource scarcity, social unrest, and the constant threat of the

unknown. But they were not alone. The group, now a united force forged through shared hardship and purpose, stood ready to face the challenges ahead.

Their collective memory of the truth, the lessons learned from the darkest depths of humanity's fall, would guide their every step. They would build a society based on trust,

compassion, and a shared commitment to a brighter future. They would create a world where hope could flourish, where the memory of the apocalypse served as a warning against the dangers of greed and manipulation, and where the

resilience of the human spirit could shine through the darkest shadows.

Lila looked out at the horizon, her gaze fixed on the faintest glimmer of light that signaled the dawning of a new day. It was a fragile hope, but it was a hope nonetheless. And in that fragile hope, she found the strength to carry on, to build, to create, to ensure that the embers of humanity would never be extinguished. The road ahead was long, but she knew that they were not walking it alone. They were walking it

together, hand in hand, with the weight of the past on their shoulders and the promise of a brighter future in their hearts.

The story was far from over. There would be new challenges to overcome, new obstacles to navigate, and new stories to tell. But as Lila looked out at the horizon, she knew that their journey was just beginning. The last dawn had passed, but the true dawn of humanity's rebirth was yet to come. And in that knowledge, she found a sense of purpose, a sense of hope, a sense of resilience that would carry them through the darkest of nights and lead them to a brighter tomorrow.

Acknowledgments

The journey to bring "The Last Dawn" to life has been fueled by the support of countless individuals. My deepest gratitude goes to my editor, Samantha

Ashwell, for their invaluable guidance and insightful feedback. Their meticulous eye and unwavering belief in the story have been instrumental in shaping this manuscript.

I am also indebted to my fellow writers and critique partners, for their insightful critiques and unwavering support. Their willingness to delve into the depths of my world and offer constructive criticism has been invaluable.

A special thank you to the people who helped with research, inspiration, etc., whose contributions have enriched the story in countless ways.

And finally, to my readers, thank you for embarking on this journey with me. Your passion for post-apocalyptic fiction inspires me to explore the depths of human resilience and the enduring power of hope.

Glossary
Glossary of Terms:
Ashfall:
The catastrophic fallout of nuclear dust and debris, covering the land in a thick layer of ash, rendering it uninhabitable.
Scavenger:
A resourceful individual who survives by foraging through the ruins of the old world, gathering resources and supplies.
Mutants:
Creatures deformed and mutated as a result of the radiation exposure, posing a constant threat to survivors.
The Consortium:
The shadowy organization responsible for orchestrating the apocalypse, seeking to control and reshape the world in their image.
The Resistance:
A loose network of survivors who fight against the Consortium's control, seeking to expose the truth and rebuild a free society.
The Zone:
A restricted area heavily controlled by the Consortium, rumored to contain advanced technology and dangerous secrets.

The Last Dawn:

A symbolic term representing the hope for a new beginning, a future free from the shadows of the past.

Author Biography

John Kuykendall is a post-apocalyptic fiction writer with a passion for exploring the depths of human resilience and the enduring power of hope in the face of adversity. Driven by a fascination with the complexities of survival, societal collapse, and the dark side of human nature, [Author Name] weaves intricate worlds and suspenseful narratives that resonate with readers seeking a thrilling escape into a world transformed.

Their debut novel, "The Last Dawn," is a testament to their commitment to crafting immersive stories that delve into the human condition in the aftermath of a catastrophic event.

John Kuykendall currently resides in Colorado, where they continue to write and explore the boundaries of storytelling, drawing inspiration from the complexities of the world around them.

Made in United States
Troutdale, OR
10/01/2024

23270679R00096